To Roisin,

THE DARK EDGE OF THINGS

Enjoy!
With all best wishes,

Freya McClements

Loe, Freya
xxx

eve

eve is an imprint of Guildhall Press dedicated to encouraging, promoting and showcasing the creativity of women authors and artists.

Published in July 2012

Guildhall Press
Unit 15, Ráth Mór Business Park
Bligh's Lane
Derry
Ireland
BT48 0LZ
(028) 7136 4413
info@ghpress.com
www.ghpress.com

Guildhall Press gratefully acknowledges the financial support of the Arts Council of Northern Ireland as a principal funder under its Annual Support for Organisations Programme.

The author asserts her moral rights in this work in accordance with the Copyright, Designs and Patents Act 1998.

Copyright © Guildhall Press/Freya McClements
ISBN: 978 1 906271 48 0

A CIP record for this book is available from the British Library.

Acknowledgements

I would like to express my heartfelt thanks to the Arts Council of Northern Ireland for the SIAP award which eventually led to this collection, to all at Guildhall Press who guided me through the process of my first publication with a kindly and supportive hand, and to my fellow writers, family and friends, who believed I could write and who gave me the inspiration to do so.

The Author

Freya McClements is a BBC journalist and literary reviewer with the *Irish Times*. In 2006 she was shortlisted for the Orange/*Northern Woman* Short Story Prize, and in 2009 she received an award from the Arts Council of Northern Ireland to write the series of short stories which became this collection. She is currently working on her first novel.

To my family

'Our interest's on the dangerous edge of things.
The honest thief, the tender murderer,
the superstitious atheist.'

Robert Browning

Foreword

Occasionally, very occasionally, a new and vibrant voice makes itself heard in the world of creative writing in Ireland; this début collection proves beyond any doubt that Freya McClements possesses one such voice. She speaks for the new generation of emergent writers; confident, individual, paying homage to the great traditions of Irish short-story writing but bringing to this classic genre an ingenuity and freshness that is all her own. It is a voice for her generation, the children of the 1980s; lyrical, resonant, at once prematurely cynical and touchingly innocent. The style is direct and economical, yet rich in attention to the minutiae of acutely observed detail. It is unique in its sense of time and place, culture and identity. *The Dangerous Edge of Things* is peopled with engaging characters and wonderfully descriptive phrases to cherish long in the memory and revisit with pleasure.

Love and lust in their many guises define this collection, from the first stirrings of adolescent desire in Last Bus to the confused innocence of advanced old age in The Girl Of My Dreams. Married love, illicit love, painful and lost love – it is all here and examined in vibrant prose that always delivers the unexpected, the charmingly witty, the almost unbearably poignant. The author spares us nothing.

These stories will stay with you, haunt you, comfort you long after you first read them. They will leave you wanting the more that must surely follow from this young and gifted writer.

The Arts Council of NI and Guildhall Press are to be lauded for their initiative in making available and accessible the first writing of one of our most exciting new voices in literary fiction.

Felicity McCall
Writer & Journalist

Contents

Laid Bare

She undresses behind a screen, jacket hung Christ-like over the back of a chair, shirt and jeans neatly folded on the hard plastic seat. Clumsy attempts at pottery litter the shelves around her, their failure illuminated by a single naked bulb hanging from a dusty shade. A mirror propped in one corner seems to mock her reservations and for a few moments she stops and studies her nakedness, sucking in her stomach and arching her back as she appraises herself. Satisfied, she hooks off knickers and pulls on a light cotton robe. A last look at her watch shows 7:30. She takes a final deep breath and pulls back the curtain.

The room has been laid out in anticipation of her entrance. A table and chair wait patiently on a platform at the front, their stark reality lit by grey daylight falling weakly from a skylight overhead. As she hesitates, she sees figures flit like moths among the cluster of easels arranged in front of her. Faces look up, their expressions palettes of excitement and embarrassment, curiosity and indifference, the low hum of their voices punctuated only by the rattle of pencils and the squeak of wood against cheap linoleum. Folding her arms in front of her, she walks towards the stage.

One of the chair legs wobbles threateningly under her weight as she takes her place, so she rises and adjusts it, then settles down once more. She has long rehearsed this moment in her mind, has come to view it as a personal epiphany, a transformation from the mundane into the exotic, her body inspiring and exciting, draped erotically on a divan and surrounded with sympathetic lighting and soft furnishings. But there is no romance in this art room, only the reality that she is simply another naked body, a specimen to be studied and reinterpreted by artistic sensibility, then joked about afterwards with spouses and friends.

'Right, class, let's get started, shall we?'

The teacher turns towards her and lets his voice fall to a reassuring whisper.

'You can put your robe on the table behind you when you're ready.'

She shrugs the cloth from her shoulders to reveal her naked form and feels the focus of the entire room fall on her body. Breathing deeply, she relishes the freedom that has come with shedding not just clothing, but a social skin, and for all the drabness of her surroundings feels a sense of achievement, of personal triumph. As she arranges her legs into the requested position, she feels a new awareness of the muscles and sinews that give them power and she deliberately flexes her limbs, enjoying her unaccustomed freedom as she takes up her pose. Her nipples harden in the cool air and she dips her head slightly to avoid eye contact, seeking to mask the embarrassment that would betray her to her audience. Instead, she focuses on the Perspex face of the clock on the back wall, trying to ignore the students that sit around her, arms outstretched as though in salutation of her courage, their thumbs and pencils measuring out the proportions of an artistic checklist of head, torso, legs, feet. One by one, the students turn to their easels and start to draw and she relaxes as she feels her consciousness blend with theirs into a single process.

Five, then ten minutes go by. Her arms begin to hurt, a dull ache blossoming to active pain as her muscles cry to be released from the unaccustomed pose. She feels a new respect for the languid nudes in art galleries, for the discomfort and dissembling which has gone into their creation. As discreetly as she can she flexes her arms ever so slightly, lifting first one palm, then the other, coaxing life back into stiff limbs. On the wall before her the clock ticks slowly on.

Only now does she allow herself to look properly at the individuals who are studying her so intently, to observe them as they observe her nakedness. Two older men sit, incongruous in suits and ties, their faces slightly flushed at the reality of her unveiling. They begin to draw self-consciously, hesitantly, as if treading warily through an alien landscape. She hears one of them call the teacher over and together they copy his demonstration, their determination almost comical as they attempt to master her outline.

She wonders if they are aroused by the naked woman in front of them or if they perceive her merely as an artistic challenge, a collection of shapes. Perhaps she is merely the ridge of an instep, the line of a thigh, the curve of a breast, her sexuality reduced to a series of asexual parts.

Only one student stands out from the others. A young man, no older than herself, dark hair falling confidently to broad shoulders. He stares at her intently as though searching for truth in the curves of her body. Around him the others sketch, look up, then sketch again, but his page remains unmarked. He catches her eye, smiles, then returns to his work. She feels her skin flush, and breathes deeply.

Eventually, the teacher interrupts: 'Time for a break.'

Relieved, she pulls on her robe and accepts the coffee offered. Sitting slightly to the side, she listens to the chatter of the class, to their excited sharing of stories, their self-conscious articulation of artistic thoughts and sensibilities. Surrounded by hidden, half-finished impressions of herself, she is curious as to how she has been depicted, her vanity piqued by the thought of how others might have perceived her.

She notices her admirer standing by the window, whispering quietly to his companions, sculpting shapes from air and imagination as though to illustrate some unseen artistic truth. He glances in her direction; she looks away, pretending to concentrate on the drink in her hands. She can feel his gaze resting heavy upon her neck, can hear him commenting to the other students. She wants to go over but checks herself. Still his presence torments her, but she forces herself to stay where she is, watching from the corner of her eye as he walks over to his easel and stands, deep in thought, before his canvas.

**

As the class resumes she sees the table has been moved to the very front of the platform and a sheet draped over it. The teacher beckons her over and points to the improvised altar. 'Can I ask you to lie on your side? Just here …'

She takes off her robe once more and, perching on the edge, swings her legs up and stretches out along the table's length. Her head rests on her arm as though awaiting a lover.

'Yes, like that, and rest your other hand along your body. Face the class … perfect.'

She watches with interest as he demonstrates how to draw the reclining nude, how to measure the body with thumb and pencil, how to note the curves and angles and break the image down into simple lines. 'Employ swift strokes,' she hears him say. 'Use the negative space to give life to your image.'

As before, the students begin enthusiastically – their eyes squinting, tongues out in concentration, a forest of pencils poised to measure her proportions.

She wonders what it would be like to have her naked form displayed on a gallery wall, to have immortality bestowed by the application of pastel and paint to a rectangle of canvas, a modern Maja to be admired or ignored by students, tourists and giggling schoolchildren. The reality, she suspects, will be a transience that ends with her image crumpled, thrown away, only one or two surviving, unseen and abandoned, until they fade away though time and apathy.

She senses her admirer staring at her again and she tilts her head ever so slightly. For a second their eyes lock and she detects the faintest outline of a smile once more upon his lips. Then, with a theatrical flourish, he begins to draw, his eyes focused solely on the page before him, his hands moving with confident, bold strokes. She stares at him intently as he recreates her on the page, each stroke a caress, a distant seduction as his gaze makes its way up her body. His pencil licks its way around her knee, traces the outline of her thigh, marks the dark wisps of hair with the briefest of strokes. She realises she is holding her breath as he explores her and wonders if the desire in her belly is apparent to those around her.

A sudden knock at the door and in an instant the spell is broken. With a furtive glance in her direction, the caretaker announces it is time to lock up. Pulling on her robe, she is almost at the changing area when she realises that noone has moved and that the students are still watching her. Discomfited, she walks quickly to the easels and surveys the pictures. A few drawings are recognisable but most look nothing like her, an improvised rendering of limbs and body parts that might be anyone. When she comes to *his* painting she stops, then laughs aloud. The page is a mess of unidentifiable shapes and dramatic strokes as if drawn by an enthusiastic but talentless child. As she walks back to the changing area, she hears the guilty laughter of the other students as they succumb to the joke.

By the time she is dressed, the room is empty save for the teacher, who wishes her an embarrassed goodnight as he hands over her fee. The corridor, too, is almost deserted, the caretaker jangling his keys impatiently to encourage the stragglers outside. Only the car park is busy, knots of students caught like shadows as they bid each other farewell. She looks for her admirer and is disappointed when he is not among them.

As she walks across the tarmac, she hears a noise and turns round but can see nothing. She continues to make her way to the car, slowly, unable to shake the sensation that there is somebody there. In the darkness, sounds blend to confuse her senses, the rustle of the leaves like a breath, the crunch of tyres on gravel concealing the pad of a footstep behind her. At the car, she stops and fumbles in her bag for the key.

Suddenly, two arms grab her waist and push her against the vehicle, kissing her violently before she can make a sound. His tongue forces his way into her mouth and she kisses back eagerly, desire fuelled by hours of restraint. His hands roam over her, fumbling at the shapes practised at the easel. Only when they pull apart do they look at each other. He smiles.

'Told you it'd be fun.'

She takes his hand. 'Come on, let's go home. The baby-sitter will be wondering where we are.'

Booklovers

It was his hair that first caught my eye. Deep auburn, studied in its wildness. He was Heathcliff on the moors, Byron at the Hellespont, head bowed in contemplation of the table of forgotten fiction at the back of the shop. My morning's work, my life's work. I watched from behind the till as he caressed each cover, as if by touch alone he could persuade it to give up its secrets. My breath caught as his long fingers passed over *Appointment in Samarra*, *A House for Mr Biswas*, *Zuleika Dobson*. He lifted *The House of Mirth* and I watched anxiously as he read the back cover before setting it down. Then, to my delight, he turned to the list of recommendations I had printed only that morning, my menu for the discerning mind. Distracted by another customer, I lost sight of him, and when I turned back, he'd gone.

Fifteen minutes later, karma, divine providence, a plot device – call it what you will – brought him to my checkout. He handed me his books. *The Postman Always Rings Twice* and *The Blank Wall*. I scanned the barcodes, then his tanned face. 'Good choices.'

He smiled as he handed me his credit card. 'They come highly recommended. It *was* you who wrote the list, wasn't it? I saw you watching me as I read it.'

His accent was Mediterranean, a melodic blend of Spanish and French. Carreras with a six-pack. I blushed and pushed my glasses further up my nose.

'You're the first person to buy one from the list. I've just finished this myself,' I said, holding up the James M Cain, then slipping it into a plastic bag as though it were a shared secret. 'They say electronic books are the future, but you can't fall in love with them, can you? You can't hold them, you can't feel their reality. I hope they never go out of date.'

He smiled again. 'Nothing classic ever goes out of date. Not books and certainly not people. Can I have …'

I was still clutching his bag. Flustered, I pushed it towards him. 'Sorry about that. Hope you enjoy them.'

**

Two days later I spotted him again, stooped once more over my recommendations.

'Why don't I give the shelves a tidy?' I called to Janet.

She pointed to a pile of books stacked haphazardly behind the till. 'Sort those out if you like.'

I took as many as I could and began restocking my way towards him. The smell of his aftershave filled the air around me as though the books themselves were made of perfumed paper and I had entered the realm of Omar Khayyam. I stopped beside my Abelard and coughed gently. 'Excuse me, can I help?'

'Um, no. I'm fine, thanks. Just browsing.'

Undaunted, I eased my grip on the pile of books in my arms until they began to sway perceptibly as though suddenly made heavy by the weight of their own erudition.

'Here, let me help you with those.' He grabbed the books just as they were about to topple onto a small child standing unawares at the *Harry Potter* display.

'You saved my life.' I nodded in the direction of the *Harry Potter* fan. 'And his.'

My conversation careered on like a driverless car.

'Did you start the James M Cain yet?'

'James M Cain? Oh, yes, now I remember. No, not yet, but it's next on my list. I'll let you know what I think, though. Promise.'

I grasped at the prospect of another encounter with the overeagerness of the habitually alone.

'Well, you know where I am. Always here.'

**

It was Friday afternoon before I saw him again. He was in the café reading a book propped against a sugar bowl. I grabbed a chocolate muffin and walked towards him.

'Mind if I sit here?'

He waved gallantly at the seat opposite. 'Please do.'

'You liked it then?' I pointed at the novel.

'It came highly recommended.' We both laughed. And in the confidence of that shared moment, he asked me out.

**

He chose The Bailey. It attracts a trendy crowd, which is why I didn't go there very often. Or at all. I squeezed my way through the people clustered around the bar and found him perched on a stool in a corner, coat draped over the empty seat beside him to ward off the anorexic PAs posing around us. He stood as I approached and greeted me with a kiss on the cheek.

'Sorry I'm late,' I said as I sat down. 'It took a while to find you.'

'Don't be silly, it's a lady's prerogative to be late. Here, I've brought you a present.'

He handed me a slim volume wrapped in layers of tissue paper.

I opened it carefully as though it might disintegrate at the slightest touch. A brightly coloured dust jacket announced *Death of a Naturalist*. My heart skipped a beat as I glanced inside. A first edition. He must have seen the look on my face but he said nothing, only smiled again. Running my hands over the cover, I savoured the feel of dry parchment, then opened it delicately, letting the pages fall where they would rather than crease the book's spine.

'It must be worth hundreds,' was all I could say.

I should have handed it back then and there but I couldn't. Not just yet. I caressed the book for a few moments longer, then offered it to him.

'I'm sorry,' I brought myself to say. 'I can't accept this. It's too much.'

'Don't be silly, it's a present. My father knew the publisher. They went to Cambridge together. Besides, books should live with those who love them and who can appreciate their artistic worth rather than their monetary value.'

'If this was mine, I'd never give it away.'

'I know. That's why it's better on your bookshelf.'

He was right. I resolved to keep it.

'But how can I repay you?'

He smiled in a way that no-one had smiled at me in years.

'You don't have to sleep with me, if that's what you think. It's a present, that's all.'

I blushed with pleasure. 'Look, can we start this again? It's beautiful, and I accept. Thank you.'

'You're welcome. Now, what'll you have to drink?'

He told me he was a part-time librarian at the National Archives, that he'd just started his doctorate on poet-revolutionaries and was studying creative writing at night. I nodded, happy just to listen, enjoying that feeling of envelopment by a male presence for the first time in years.

As people drifted in and out of the bar, he told me of his struggles and hopes, of times down-and-out in Madrid and Vienna, of travels to Istanbul with an eccentric relative, of a night spent in a deserted mission in Mexico. Eventually, he stopped. 'I'm sorry. I must be boring you silly. I tend to over-romanticise a bit. Too much Keats.'

'No, no,' I protested. 'Literature is the greatest thing in the world.' I looked down at the bar. 'Well, one of.'

As I ordered another drink, I thought how much I wanted to kiss him.

He walked me home along Nassau Street. It was a warm, clear night and the wine had me skipping along, my shoes in my hand. As we came to Dame Street, I flung out my arms to embrace the life pulsing around me. 'I love nights like this in Dublin, when history and literature come to life. It's intoxicating.'

'Do you find me intoxicating?'

We had come to my bus stop. The 46A waited, its passengers illuminated like figures in a Hopper painting, lonely hearts waiting for a chance that never comes.

I stood on tiptoe and kissed him. 'Very.'

'Do you want to come back to my place?' he asked.

I smiled at the Mills & Boon moment. 'I'd love to.'

**

I examined his sitting room while he went out to put on the kettle. Its centrepiece was a cast-iron fireplace next to a window seat on which cushions and pages of poetry lay scattered as though Oscar Wilde had just left. Against the walls were ceiling-high bookcases, their shelves so laden it seemed as if the weight of one more volume might send them crashing to the ground. It was a room that spoke of character, of lonely nights composing sonnets by firelight and where inspiration fell from the shelves into one's dreams. Piled on a table beside me were plays by Lorca, poems by Neruda, novels by Marquez, evocative titles that spoke to me of a man seeking to transcend mortality through the power of words.

Carefully, I eased a copy of *Homage to Catalonia* off a shelf and scanned the title page. To my surprise, I found that it, too, was a first edition.

'You've found my collection, then?' He handed me a cup, and reached up to prise a book from the tightly packed shelf. 'I'm particularly proud of this one. *Rebelión en la Granja*. The first Spanish edition of *Animal Farm*.'

'It's beautiful. They're all beautiful.' I was a pilgrim who had stumbled upon a hidden shrine. 'Where did you get them?'

'From my mother. She's Spanish. Her father, my grandfather, was a lecturer at the University of Barcelona. Franco's thugs murdered him in 1937. The day after they killed Lorca.'

I clutched the revelation to me as yet more evidence of his romantic pedigree. 'She must be very proud of you.'

'She died when I was little.' He put his arm round my waist and kissed me. 'But I'd like to think she would have been.'

**

Our romance was everything I'd hoped for. We were passionate and bohemian, rewriting the rules of love as we gorged ourselves on our literary lifestyle. We would lie in bed, scribbling in notebooks, on printer paper, on beer mats, whatever came to hand. Then we'd read our work aloud before reaching for each other again. Sometimes when I was at work, he'd come and sit in the café simply to watch me. He told me he was writing a novel about me. I was to be his muse, his Laura, his Beatrice. One day, the supervisor caught us kissing, my lover's hand fumbling at my clothes. I was reprimanded but didn't care. I had learned to crave the erotic feel of paper on skin, the smell of ink and sex. We kissed in the science section and he went down on me in the toilets, my back a wall's width away from the out-of-print books. At night, when it was quiet, we would go to the rare-book room and I would show him beautiful volumes, ancient atlases and first editions. They were our aphrodisiac. And once we had inhaled their scent, we would race back to his apartment and imagine they surrounded us as we made love.

That was how it came about. We were lying in bed one night, my head resting on the crook of his arm as I lazily explored him with my fingers.

'What if we took one?' he asked, gazing at the lightshade above his head.

I looked up, suddenly frightened. 'What do you mean?'

'Well, those books, most of them just sit there like creatures in cages and are never looked at, never read. Nobody's going to buy them; they've become like museum pieces, their purpose forgotten. We could look after them, make them live again.'

'You mean steal them?'

He pulled me down and kissed me. 'No. Just borrow them. For a night or two. Think what it would be like to own one of those volumes, even for a few hours. We'd leave them back before anyone noticed.'

I said I would think it over but I knew from the very beginning that I'd say yes. Later that night, he held me close and murmured titles in my ear like kisses.

**

It was too easy. The next night, I waited until the shop was about to close and then made my way to the rare-book room. One of the supervisors was replacing a volume on the shelf and I gave a garbled story about checking an order. Convinced I'd given myself away, I contemplated explanations, pleas for clemency, but she merely nodded and returned to her task as I busied myself at the computer, loitering until I was certain she'd left.

I went over to the shelves. We'd decided it would be safer to choose a cheaper volume for our first attempt, so I picked a thin volume of Browning's poetry. Easier to hide. Taking a last look round to check nobody was there, I stuffed it into the waistband of my skirt and walked calmly towards the door. I was frightened but excited by the feel of the book against my skin, by a sense of danger that I realised had been absent from my life for far too long. I felt like a heroine in a novel, a twenty-first-century Moll Flanders. I imagined the moment my lover would take out the book, how we would sit naked on the bed together turning the pages.

That image sustained me as I transferred the book into my bag and walked towards the front door. The shutters were half-down, keys in the lock. It was Mr Philips himself who was waiting to let us out. As he looked at me, I felt panic rise in my throat, then he simply wished me goodnight. A cheery farewell, and I was outside. Free. I wanted to stop and drink draughts of intoxicating air, but I forced myself to walk slowly up the street until I was out of view.

It was an unusually warm autumn evening, the street crowded with students and shop workers hurrying home. At the top of Grafton Street, people stood watching the street entertainers and a sudden burst of laughter erupted as a little girl jumped in response to a human statue that had suddenly come to life. I turned and ran all the way back to my lover's lair.

He was waiting for me at the door. I kissed him breathlessly, fired with my own audacity.

'You did it, I can tell.'

I took him by the hand and led him to the bed, then proudly handed him the book.

He opened it reverentially, held it like a heart surgeon cradling a human organ. Reaching over, he kissed my open mouth. And for that instant we became Rodin's lovers.

**

From then on we were addicted. I made sure to borrow only the rarest books, ones that were seldom looked for, and I was careful not to build up a pattern, taking them on different days and leaving them back the next morning.

'If we get caught, the papers will call us a literary Bonnie and Clyde,' he joked one night.

I took a first edition of *Treasure Island* from his hands. 'I don't care how all this ends … as long as we're together.'

He pulled me close, his lips soft against my ear. 'They have a *Ulysses*. In its original Paris binding. Only a thousand ever printed.'

I nodded. 'It's worth a fortune. How'd you find out about it? We never broadcast that one.'

He laughed. 'The first evening we sneaked in, remember? It was in the cabinet above your head. Wouldn't it be fun to own it, just for an evening?'

I knew even then that I would steal it.

**

The theft seemed to awaken something deep within me, a lust that could not be satisfied until it had consumed us both. Eventually we lay at peace, and I watched him turn the pages again and again, poring over the book as though it held the secret to all of life's mysteries. When he had finished I insisted on wrapping it in tissue paper and putting it back in the bookcase for safety's sake. I slid it onto the shelf beside *Death of a Naturalist*. I grazed its spine with my fingertips and drew them briefly to my lips, then turned towards him. He held me close as we slept like spoons in our bed of paper.

Morning sunshine roused me. I rolled over, seeking the comfort of his sleeping form, and it was only after several minutes I realised he wasn't there. I glanced at the clock: 6:52. He never went out that early. I got up and wandered into the bathroom. His toothbrush was gone, his razor, too. I rushed into the kitchen to find his computer missing. His jacket no longer hung from the back of the chair where he'd thrown it the night before. Frantically I flung open the wardrobe, pulled out every drawer in our bedroom. Empty. My lover was gone, but I tried his mobile anyway. Switched off. I threw my phone down on the bed in frustration but missed and sent it skating across the floor to crash against the bottom of the bookcase. As I picked it up I saw the gap on the shelf.

At least he'd left me the Heaney. I picked it up and sat back on the bed, cradling it on my lap, then opened it carefully. A bright blue cover peeked out from beneath the dust jacket. Tears of relief overwhelmed me. He hadn't noticed. I dried my eyes with my sleeve and ran my fingers over the title, as if to reassure myself it was real. *Ulysses* by James Joyce. Paris, 1922. I wrapped it up again and tucked it carefully into my bag, then clipped on my name badge and walked towards the door.

Happily Ever After

I park out of sight and wait. In the distance, church bells toll the day's passing. Across the road, teenagers lounge against a wall in the early evening sunshine, their heads bowed over mobile phones, fingers dancing as they text friends a street away. A girl in school uniform kisses the boy beside her for what seems like minutes, then returns to the ice cream that has dripped over her hand. A builder who is fitting a new sign to the shop front beside me looks in to see my legs. I open a newspaper and pretend to read.

Minutes pass before I catch sight of him in the rear-view mirror, sidling his way towards me through the passing shoppers. Inches from the car, he is stopped by a woman in a suit and I hear their muffled voices beat against the glass.

'Who was that?' I ask as he gets in.

He scans the street before replying and decides not to risk a kiss. 'No-one, just an old neighbour. Nothing to worry about. Let's go.'

I ease the car into gear and sense him relax as we pull away from the row of shops.

'Did you see the kids across the road? When I was their age, we used to go to the park to do that sort of stuff. We thought we were so grown-up. I remember Paul McKinney declaring he would love me forever because I gave him a handjob beside the swings.'

27

The image catches his interest. 'Lucky boy. Where is he now?'

'God knows, but I doubt he's pining away for me somewhere.'

I place my hand in his lap, removing it only to change gear. I know he is uncomfortable, conscious of the cars and pedestrians that might observe us, might recognise us as we make our way through the town-centre traffic.

'How long have we got?'

'A few hours. I said I had an evening meeting. What about Brian?'

'He thinks I'm at a leaving-do for one of the girls in advertising. I told him not to wait up. What if Sandra rings?'

'She won't.'

'Because she trusts you?'

'Because she doesn't care.'

When we get to the hotel, he deals with the check-in while I loiter suspiciously by the lift, a twenty-first-century woman with twentieth-century morals. Only when the door is firmly closed behind us do I let him kiss me. By the time we reach the room I am too aroused to notice its drab banality, the smell of someone else's lovemaking still pervading the small space that is temporarily ours. We used to take each other's clothes off, but now we just strip and get into bed. I am struck by how quickly we have settled into the hurried rituals of what has become an affair.

'What do you want to do?' he asks me breathlessly.

I don't answer, content to let him take charge, and he grips me tightly. Afterwards, we lie with our limbs tangled together like runners who have collapsed at a finishing line.

I sense the change in him before it occurs, can hear the cogs whirling in his brain as he disengages from me and prepares to face the reality outside. As he gets up he runs his hands roughly over me, like a farmer examining a prize ewe. Irritated by his act of proprietorship, I walk to the bathroom in silence. He follows and tries to kiss me again, but I avoid his embrace and start to brush my teeth.

'It's after eleven. You need to wash your face. You smell of sex.'

I drop him downtown and watch as he walks towards his car. A snake shedding its skin, he seems to change with every step he takes away from me. As he reaches his BMW I see him take out the aftershave he keeps hidden in his jacket pocket and sprinkle some on. I absolve you in the name of the Father, and the Son, and the Holy Spirit.

**

It had started so carelessly. A drink after work with the firm's newest clients, banter that turned to whispers until we were the only two left, neither as drunk as we'd pretended to be. In the darkness of the office he'd put his hands all over me. I was the one who produced the condom. 'It's a long time since I've worn one of these,' he'd said as I rolled it on.

Later we agreed the rules that would give a moral veneer to our betrayal. No texts, no phone calls to either home. A Monday-to-Friday betrayal, weekends off. Sex not love, friendship not commitment. A bit of fun for as long as we both wanted it. Nobody would ever know.

**

Brian was in bed when I got home. Still invigorated from the sex, I made myself a bowl of cornflakes in the kitchen while I debated whether a shower would give me away. In the end I washed hastily in the bathroom, then tiptoed in and slid under the covers as quietly as I could. He shifted in his sleep and put his arm round me. 'Good night?' he whispered.

'Mmm, sorry I'm so late. Jenny had a bit too much to drink and I had to take her home.' I delivered the line I'd rehearsed all the way home. 'Did you and Lauren have a nice night?'

'Great. We took her bike to the park and then came home and watched her new DVD. I had to carry her up when it was over.'

I waited until he settled back into sleep, the duvet moving up and down reassuringly with his breathing. I felt no guilt, only excitement.

**

After that first betrayal it got easier. I became committed to my work, going in early, coming home late, fucking on desks in deserted offices as we prayed that nobody would walk in. After a few months we became braver, sneaking away for extended lunches in hotel rooms or parking in deserted lay-bys like randy teenagers. That winter I carried my duplicity with me – to Lauren's nativity play, to dinner at my parents, even to our anniversary dinner. My reality became multifaceted and multi-layered, my life lit by my darkest moments.

**

We'd been seeing each other for almost a year when I realised he had broken all the rules. On a rare evening together we drove to the beach at Kinnego. It's the sort of place where couples go to be alone, where a priest might take his housekeeper on a discreet walk. It was November, the freezing water iron-grey, so we had the place to ourselves. When his phone rang I instinctively turned back towards the car, half-listening to his muffled excuses as he lied about why he would be late home again. Suddenly he stopped and pulled me to him, squeezing my arms and kissing me hard. I extricated myself with difficulty and instinctively looked around me, checking the beach, the hills, the car park for witnesses.

'Be careful. Somebody could have seen us.'

'I don't care. I can't do this anymore. I want to be with you.'

I laughed uneasily. 'You know that's not going to happen. You know the rules.'

I started to walk away, but he grabbed me, more forcefully this time.

'Sod the rules. I love you.'

I avoided his kiss. 'Say that again and it's over.'

He looked at me in disbelief. 'How can you be so cold, so clinical? Does nothing we've done mean anything to you? I want to be with you.'

'What about your wife and kids?'

'I don't care. It's you I want.'

'Look, if I'd wanted a deep and meaningful relationship I'd have found someone deep and meaningful to have it with. I've already got a husband. This is about sex, and if you can't cope with that, end it. Now I have to go.'

I wrenched myself free from his grip and hurried over to the car. We drove back in silence.

That night he was beside me, his breathing hoarse and rapid, his body pressing like a knife into the small of my back. His arm had curled itself around me like a serpent, protecting our unborn child, the fruit of our infidelity. My only thought was escape and I tried to get up, but his grip tightened and I felt his hand encircling my throat. I woke with a shriek. Brian was beside me, stroking my hair, soothing me.

'Ssshhh, it's only a nightmare.'

I lay down again and he held me, his body folded around mine reassuringly. But I couldn't sleep, couldn't lose the fear of the baby clinging to my insides like some demonic parasite. It had to end.

When I get to work next morning he is there, perched on the end of my desk, sharing a joke with Colette, its punch line lost on me. When nobody is looking I lead him into an empty office. He tries to slide his hand up my skirt, but I push him away. 'Cut it out. What the hell are you doing?'

'It's alright, I told them we had a meeting. I wanted to see you.'

'I'm touched. You've seen me, now go.'

He puts his hand to my face and strokes my cheek. 'Look, if this is about yesterday, I'm sorry. I don't know what came over me. Can we forget about it and start again?'

Against my better judgement I let him kiss me. He puts his arms round me and despite myself I relax into what has become a familiar embrace.

'What about this afternoon? I'll say I've got a doctor's appointment.'

Something makes me decline. 'I can't, I've actually got the dentist,' I lie. As I leave the room, I am struck by how hurt he looks.

That night I get Brian to take Lauren to her piano lesson and I pour a glass of wine while I run a bath. When the water is almost too hot to bear, I immerse myself in it. The flickering candle by the side of the bath reminds me of votive offerings in darkened churches. Bless me, Father, for I have sinned. Only I don't want redemption or forgiveness. I want escape.

**

On Saturday morning the phone rings. He has a cover story ready if Brian answers about an emergency at work and I have to play along, heart thumping in case he suspects anything. I agree to meet him in our usual hotel, where I go through the familiar motions. I am cold, my body rigid as he makes love to me. But my passivity only excites him all the more and I realise for the first time how much I despise him. His weight presses down as he grunts on top of me, the sour smell of his sweat clogging my nostrils. I close my eyes and ask God to rid me of him, to remove him from my life.

When he is finished I look at my watch. 'I have to go. Brian will be wondering where I am.'

He mistakes the flatness in my voice for reluctance and puts his arms round me.

'I know. I wish you didn't have to go, either. I wish you could stay with me.'

His hold tightens like a noose around my neck. I remember my dream and throw the words out like stones.

'I had a nightmare the other night. I was pregnant with your child.'

'Would that be so bad?'

I remove myself from his grasp and look at him with undisguised contempt. 'Yes, it would. I already have a child.'

My clothes lie crumpled on the floor. I throw the garments on and take my shoes in my hand.

'Look, this is over. I'm leaving now and I never want to see you again. Not ever.'

He clutches my arm as I reach for the door, pulling me back. 'I won't let you do this. I'll tell Brian, I swear to Christ I will.'

I hear a lock turn in a cell door and I try not to fall. 'So what happens next? We keep going like this?'

'If need be. But I love you, no matter what you say or think.'

There is a look of triumph in his eyes, in the smile that has formed upon his lips. And I realise for the first time that insanity has taken hold, the kind of insanity that comes from failure and desperation. And at that moment, too, I realise he'll tell Brian anyway, every sordid detail. Fear encases me in ice and from then on I feel no warmth.

That night I sit up late and wonder if I could kill him. If I could do it and get away with it. I consider ways and times and places, car crashes and carbon-monoxide poisoning and tragic accidents like falling down stairs. Never do I consider its morality, only its practicalities. The problem, I decide, is that I've been too indiscreet. Too many people have seen us in hotel lobbies and car parks, in out-of-the-way bars and the sauna at the gym. All it would take would be one slip, one oversight, and it would be over.

Or I could tell Brian myself. I rehearse how to throw myself on his mercy and beg forgiveness: for the sake of our love, for the sake of our child, for the sake of the scandal that will otherwise engulf us. But I cannot convince even myself.

The phone wakes me the next morning. It's Siobhan, asking if she can come over. She's been crying. I meet her at the door and we go out to the garden. She tries not to look at me as she speaks.

'Look, I don't know what was going on between you and Neil, and to be honest it's none of my business, but I thought you should hear this from me first.'

I wait, my heart racing.

'Neil's dead. Apparently he fell down the stairs at home last night and broke his neck. His wife called an ambulance but there was nothing they could do. It's on the local news. I'm sorry, but I thought someone should tell you.'

She watches as I arrange my face into a semblance of sadness and I wonder if she knows.

Brian is awake when I return to bed. 'You'll never guess what happened to one of our clients. You know Neil …'

**

Later, my husband and daughter sit at the breakfast table chatting idly about the day to come. I watch them as I pour milk onto Lauren's bowl of Coco Pops and wonder if they will ever know how I have betrayed and saved them, that my prayers have been answered by a god no more perfect than ourselves, only more powerful. I will not trouble my family's certainties, their belief in a world of right and wrong, good and bad. No, better to keep quiet, to let my secret die with him and let the rumours ripple the pond of life for a few short months.

Homecoming

I pull the heavy wooden gate closed behind me and walk quickly towards the bus stop, my breath solid against the cold air of early morning.

The High Street is busy despite the early hour, the remnants of yesterday drifting through the streets to trouble the possibilities of the day to come. The survivors of a college ball queue at a kebab van, a girl in an emerald-green gown at the hatch. She hands a carton to a tuxedo-clad figure slumped on the steps behind her and sits down heavily next to him. For a second, her boyfriend looks at the food as though it's an ill-conceived experiment, then empties his stomach over her shoes. The girl in the green dress stares blankly at the pool of orange vomit spreading about her feet and begins to eat, her plastic fork stabbing mechanically at the food. I remind myself to tell you about it when I get home.

At the bus stop I check my watch. Five to four. Leaning against the crenellated wall of the college, I feel protected, as though granted sanctuary by some ancient academic charter. The streetlights guard like sentries, their halogen eyes staring intently at the buildings opposite, at the students who pass by, dresses stained and bow ties askew, hands clutching half-empty pint glasses. The solitary revellers walk unsteadily through their blurred world, lacking the confidence of those who lean on each other for support as they make their way home to shared beds.

Without the streetlights it could be the fourteenth century. The night erases modernity, transforming the quaint carvings on the college walls into ominous heralds of a different age. Tributes to famous scientists adorn the walls of University College opposite and as I await I imagine Newton, Hooke and Boyle taking the air in wigs and tails, their gowns trailing authority and veneration behind them.

I hail the bus and its dark warmth envelops me as I show the driver my pass, climb the stairs and take a seat. Automatically, I take out my phone, then put it away again. Too early. I don't want to wake you.

My coat folded into a makeshift pillow, I rest my head against the cool of the window and watch the landmarks flash past like lecture slides. I relish the gathering sense of freedom as each mile brings me further away, past colleges and shops, through sleeping suburbs and onto the open road at last. I know the signs well by now. Beaconsfield. Amersham. Slough. Each one tempting me to places I will never visit. Turning my head, I search for comfort on the hard seat.

The couple in front of me are kissing enthusiastically, the way we did in the beginning. Ours was a credit-card courtship, an orgy of dinner dates and weekends away until the student loan ran out and reality intervened. It was then you asked me to move in with you. To save money. A typically unromantic proposal. I remember waking up that first morning and seeing you asleep beside me, your arm thrown proprietorially over my breasts.

I ask you to come to Oxford, but you never do. You're always broke, or can't get away from work, or have 'something on', some unspecified task that remains forever uncompleted. In reality, you feel threatened and hide your fears behind talk of 'posh friends' and stuffy evenings talking 'bullshit'. I send you job ads from the local paper, but nothing is ever quite right, ever quite you, so I stop looking. I've never told you this, but there was one guy here I liked. Simon. A music student in the year above. He took me to *La Bohème*, the sort of thing you'd scoff at. I agreed to 'coffee afterwards' and we fondled half-heartedly on the sofa before I made my excuses and left. He'd made me realise it was only ever you I wanted. You don't know that either.

When I wake, the bus is nearly at the airport. Among the first to dismount, I hurry straight for the lift that leads to the terminal. Somehow the Belfast plane is always the furthest away, its designated departure lounge jutting out over the tarmac like a bastion of glass, a defence against the passengers coming and going. I find a seat by the window and take out my book as planes land and take off before me. I've been fascinated by their gaudy tails ever since childhood, a legacy of the time when I would lie in bed and gaze at the map of the world that my once-proud parents had glued to the ceiling. Back then, I'd imagine all the places I would someday go. Baja California. Sulawesi. The Ruyuku Islands. Brightly coloured shapes made more beautiful by the promise of an exotic name. Now I travel home to you.

I always pride myself on waiting for the final call, relishing the last of my coffee as the other passengers cram towards the gate. Row 24, seat A. Once on board, I disturb a wealthy-looking couple whose ample bodies block me from the window. The woman tuts, hands clasping an expensive handbag in jewellery-laden fingers. Later, she has to be told to put it under the seat before take-off. Once airborne, she takes out the in-flight magazine and summons the stewardess to order a drink.

I reopen my own book and remove the letter tucked inside. An offer to study for my Master's, plus some teaching hours. Reply by Monday. In the past, you've suggested

Magee, even Queen's as a compromise, dropping alternatives into my ears like slow poison. We could get a place in Belfast, you said, and I wouldn't have to travel so much or be so tired. It would be easier in the long run. We could look after each other.

I look out the window. White-topped waves crest the water below, a container ship stark and solitary against the immensity of the sea. I wonder if its crewmen have noticed the aeroplane passing high above them or if their only focus is the sea, their sole preoccupation survival.

I check my watch. Nearly seven. I close my eyes and think of you asleep in our bed, your body encroaching on the space where I should lie. I ache with the memory of you on my skin and I wonder if you are dreaming of me now, anticipating my arrival.

The plane's sudden descent jolts me awake. An expanse of blue water and then we are over the shore, the sand merging into a receding hairline of dunes that transforms before my eyes into endless green fields. Tiny cows and hedges flash past, a presbyterian landscape where everything has its place. Or almost everything.

The passengers spill into Arrivals, where a bright-blue expanse of Ulster carpet stretches out to meet us. Welcome to a form of home. I look round, just in case, then tell myself not to be silly. I've always told you not to come, and you've always agreed. At the bus stop, I pace up and down, energised by the familiarity of my surroundings. I am nearly there.

Home. The streets have that fresh, early-morning feel as if life has paused to wonder at what the day might bring. I rush down the road and across the square, smiling in recognition at a passing postman. Hurrying on, I turn the corner and see our door.

There's no answer. I feel in my pocket for my key but I'm distracted by the state of the sitting room. The curtains have been left open and the room looks dishevelled, empty beer glasses littering the floor, blankets and pillows piled up on the sofa. For a moment, I wonder if you are asleep underneath the detritus and I knock on the window. Nothing stirs. I peer through the glass, searching for signs of life, but all I see is my plant on the mantelpiece, dead. You have forgotten to water it. Rubbish lies piled up in the hearth, a tiny altar to your sloth. Our house feels abandoned and neglected – as if nobody has lived there in months. I turn and walk quickly down the path.

The park where I decide to wait for you is built on a hill overlooking the city, and from a graffitied bench I pick out familiar landmarks. My old school, the cathedral, the City Walls. I follow the river as it winds its leisurely way northwards, carrying a cruise ship out to sea and on to somewhere new, somewhere more exciting. Below in the Bogside, a team of men perched on ladders are repainting Free Derry Corner while a tour group takes pictures from which the misery and suffering have been edited out by time.

I see you at last, walking up the hill on the other side of the road, a holdall slung over your back like a crumpled shell. I wave, but you don't see me, so I follow you like an amateur spy as you walk without urgency towards our house. I see you search for your keys in your familiar, fumbling way, then you go inside and I lose sight of you. I picture you going into the kitchen and turning on the kettle. A few minutes later, your shadow comes into the sitting room and the television flickers to life.

If I walk up the path now, you'll see me. I imagine you opening the door and kissing me on the step, then ushering me inside and shutting out the world. Tempted, my hand rests on the gate. You're probably already stretched out on the sofa, the remote in your hand. I creep up and peer in at you, watch your peculiar mannerisms, the way you brush your hair back from your eyes, the way you fiddle idly with the watch I bought you. Eventually, you fall asleep, arms wrapped around yourself like a child seeking comfort. I take the key out of my pocket and drop it gently through the letter box onto the unseen mat. With one last look through the window, I turn and walk back the way I came.

The Girl Of My Dreams

He sees Patricia waiting for him, just as she's done every Thursday since that first afternoon, the day the bomb fell in the square. He can still remember the deafening clang as the 2000lb shell struck the cobblestones, then the ominous silence that had followed. He'd waited for it to explode and shatter the normality around it, had waited for it to tear through his flesh and hurl him into darkness. Then he'd seen her and he'd been struck by the calm of the young woman in a nurse's uniform, gently ushering people away from the heavy metal cylinder. Later, once the bomb had been defused, he'd asked her to a dance. Now, as he walks towards her, he waves jauntily.

Margaret waves back as she watches her husband cross the road. In better times they'd often meet here, and she smiles as she recalls the warm evenings when she'd walk to the station to surprise him and she would stroll home on the arm of her handsome husband in his blue BEA uniform. Even now he will rarely be seen in anything other than a suit and tie, the scent of cologne and the triangle of silk in his top pocket a homage to his younger self. As he reaches her, she has to help him onto the footpath.

He stumbles and grabs her arm to steady himself. 'You look beautiful in that dress, really beautiful. I've always liked it.' He pauses. 'We bought it in Camden, didn't we? Or was it Kensington? One of the shops on the High

43

Street. You'd saved up your coupons, remember? To buy the material. You spent all that Sunday making it.'

She keeps her voice deliberately light. 'I can't remember. It was so long ago. Actually, if you think about it, it couldn't be the same dress. How would it fit me after all these years?'

He'd watched her lay the fabric on the table, smoothing it down carefully before pinning on the pattern. She'd taken the scissors and began to cut, the blade like the prow of a ship easing its way confidently through the bright ocean of material. It was a warm afternoon and music from next door's wireless seeped in through the open windows. He'd slipped his hands round her waist and tried to dance, but she'd laughed and swatted him away. 'Stop it. You know I have to get this finished.'

She takes his arm on the uneven cobbles as they turn down Elm Row, the uncertainty underfoot paralleling the doubt growing in her mind. Last weekend he didn't know their neighbour of twenty years and on Thursday he hadn't recognised the postman. At the time, she'd dismissed such mistakes as the forgetfulness that comes with age, but she can't explain the references to places they've never been, to people she's never heard of. She wants to question him, to force him to acknowledge reality but she is afraid to articulate her fears lest she breathes life into them. Silently, she leads him to the church gate.

Nervously, she steps inside. The courtyard is crowded with men in uniform, parents, wives, children in their best clothes. It's the first time he's been back since the war ended. Too many reminders. But he had to come for the unveiling. A man on crutches hobbles towards him and extends his hand, his face badly scarred. Bill Johnston. A rower who'd lost a leg at Anzio. They walk slowly towards the memorial. A simple list of names. He looks for Albert

Fanshaw. Killed in action. France, 1944. Best bowler the school ever had. One of the first to die on D-day. Shot before he reached the beach.

She stands to one side and listens as he points out familiar names on the plaque, recounting the stories he has told so many times. A history buffed and polished like the brass before him, tales of men who need never grow old, never succumb to the faults and follies of those left behind nor suffer the slow humiliation that comes with age. Eventually, she has to hurry him. 'Come on or we'll be late.'

She leads him past the pews to their usual spot on the left, just beside the stained-glass window of St Michael. Their row is empty. She remembers when the church would be packed on a Sunday, but now most of the congregation is made up of elderly couples like themselves. The vicar makes a point of greeting everyone by name, and she notices the exuberance with which her husband extends his hand, gripping the vicar's arm and smiling broadly.

As the vicar congratulates him he sees the door of the chapel open. His bride walks towards him, a veiled beauty in a wedding dress of faded white. He stands at the altar and watches her, marvelling at the grace and elegance with which she moves. She will soon be his.

'You're a lucky man,' his father whispers in his ear. 'You look after her, son.' He will never forget those words.

She takes her place beside him, and for the first time since the war began, he no longer feels a weight pressing on his shoulders. He reaches out and squeezes her hand. 'I love you. I want this to be the start of the rest of our lives.'

She wonders who he is talking to, what he is seeing. 'What did you say, dear?'

Confusion momentarily clouds his thoughts but he

will not let it distract him, not on this day of all days. 'Patricia, I've booked the loveliest little hotel for us. It's right out in the country, away from everyone, just you and me. It's by a lake.'

'Who's Patricia?' She feels like a thief trying to steal her way inside his head. 'Is she here, is she somebody you used to know? Who is she?'

He listens carefully to the vicar's words and solemnly repeats the pledge, then slides the ring onto her finger. He kisses her when bidden, smiling broadly at the guests as he leads her down the aisle towards the future.

She realises he can't hear her, that something is playing over and over again in his mind like a broken cinema reel. She grabs his shoulders and stares into his eyes, searching for recognition. 'Who's Patricia? I'm your wife: Margaret. We got married in 1956. You remember? My father gave me away. My sister was a bridesmaid. The RAF chaplain was called Reverend MacLeod; he had a thick Scottish accent. You remember that, don't you?'

Around them the tiny congregation has started to sing. It reminds her of their wedding service, their families and friends crowded into the small church near the base. Her father had been opposed to the match, convinced that he was too old and she too young, but she was determined to get married and relished the thought of being a pilot's wife when her school friends were still walking out with village boys. They'd left for Aden the year after, in '57. All she'd seen before they'd left were the newsreels of Suez, but it turned out to be nothing like that. She had her own house, and a maid, and every day she and the other wives would sunbathe or swim at the club in the Gold Mohur hotel, before drinks at the bar or the officers' mess.

**

The next morning she makes an appointment with the doctor. As she telephones, she notices a small model plane on the windowsill opposite. Another new habit, abandoning things in unusual places. He'd made it for their son, a child's toy so intricately constructed that it was a thing of beauty. Picking it up, she spins the tiny wheels with her fingertip. William had tried so hard to make it fly, launching it from tree tops and bedroom windows in the vain hope that height and wind would give it life. In the end, he'd attached a string to the undercarriage and pulled it behind him, pretending he was a pilot like his father. She wonders if her husband remembers it now.

He shuffles in as she does the hoovering, puzzled by the medical paraphernalia which has accumulated in the house. He says nothing, just sits in his chair by the window and watches the birds fight over titbits left on the sill. He doesn't say much, worried lest his words cause offence to the figure tidying the room. He wonders when Patricia will be back and if they can afford a housemaid on his salary.

They still go to church, and on visits to her sister, and on familiar walks every day. It was the doctor's suggestion. Keep familiar routines for as long as possible. One evening she takes him to the opera. He listens to the music as if enraptured and he is once more the man she married, but when it ends and they stand in the street with the hum of life all around them, she finds it harder to accept who he has become. The pull of the past is growing stronger as the disease creeps through his body and she knows that one day she will lose him forever.

'Who's Patricia?' she asks him casually, immediately feeling guilt at the obvious confusion on his face, at the pain she has caused. Let him keep his secret to the end, until illness has eroded his defences and deprived him of the ability to dissemble.

She has been luckier than most wives. There has never been a hint of an affair, and aside from his pipe and the odd whiskey, her husband has been remarkably free of vice. Still, suspicion has crept its way into her thoughts over the years, has prompted her to search the house for clues. But he has never had a locked drawer or private desk where revelations might lie hidden, and she finds nothing in the boxes of papers in the attic beyond old bank statements and dusty Christmas decorations.

He becomes more difficult and the doctors tell her she may have to consider care. One morning she is at the sink when she feels him behind her, his arms encircling her as though to hold on to the last vestiges of a slowly disintegrating present. She turns and sees eyes in which confusion has replaced awareness. Taking him by the hand, she leads him to the sofa and, sitting down, tells him she loves him, over and over, until he falls asleep in her arms.

Later, she finds him staring at their wedding photograph as though it were a puzzle, a snapshot of someone else's life. 'I see the picture. I see it and I know it's a wedding and it must be our wedding, but I can't remember it. I just can't remember.'

She has no words to reassure him, so says nothing. Instead, she watches as he feels at the side of his chair for his stick, then slowly walks over to her. Taking his arm, she allows him to lead her around the room to a tune only he can hear.

'I remember the first night I took you dancing. I couldn't believe it. I'd given up hope and then suddenly there you were. I was the luckiest man on earth that night.' She buries her head in his shoulder so he won't see her cry.

**

The next day she comes home from the supermarket to find the house empty, his overcoat gone from the stand in the hall. Rushing into the street, she sees a neighbour is at his front door waving goodbye to his daughter and son-in-law.

'My husband, have you seen him?' she shouts.

The neighbour mentions a taxi but before he can elaborate she has disappeared back inside. Phone book in hand, she calls every firm on the list and eventually the right one answers.

**

He opens the gate and walks with slow deliberation between the narrow rows where the weeds cluster like mourners around the older headstones. At the second-last row he stops, turns towards the plot in front of him, then starts to tidy it slowly, putting the old flowers in the bin before rinsing and refilling the vase. He has brought roses and arranges them carefully before the small headstone. Satisfied, he pulls his coat closer. Sits on the bench opposite. Closes his eyes. Surrenders to his memories.

It is dark by the time she arrives. The graveyard is old and overgrown and she has to beat back foliage from the gate as she enters. Occasionally she loses her footing on the tree roots and moss that have taken possession of the narrow paths but she continues to feel her way between the rows of stone and grass. Eventually, she finds him on a bench in the farthest corner, keeping watch over a headstone. With difficulty she makes out the inscription.

Patricia Graham 1919–1942
Stella Graham 1940–1942
Beloved wife and daughter.

She takes his hand. He is cold but alive. She wraps his coat around her legs, then sits down beside him, her head resting gently on his shoulder.

The moon casts shadows over the names before them and in the imperfect darkness she feels him shiver. She takes a handkerchief from her handbag and raises it to his nose and mouth and holds it there. In a few minutes she feels him relax. She settles herself closer against him. She will look at the stars just a little while longer.

Last Bus

I turn off the pavement and duck into a narrow alleyway, leaving behind streets suffocating in the fuggy glow of the week before Christmas. The whole seasonal thing bores me, too much fake happiness and distant relatives trying to kiss you. And I hate the zombies who go Christmas shopping, eyes glazed with desperation and greed as they follow each other from shop to shop, and the way they tut at you when they're the ones with the big bags that thump against you as they barge past.

Holding my breath, I make my way through the urine-stained passageway as quickly as I can, breathing out heavily when at last I reach the sanctuary of the bus station. Not that I like buses, either, mind you. The smell of diesel always makes me feel sick, the cloying way it infiltrates your mouth and nose until you feel like you've been drinking it. Two more years until I'm able to drive and you'll not see me near public transport ever again. And I hate the people, the depressing crowd trying to force their way on board just to get first choice of a patch of badly upholstered seats.

My bus waits at the end of the row. The lights are on but the doors are closed. I know from experience the driver will have locked it while he warms his hands around a cup of tea in the office. Reluctantly, I sit down on the metal seat opposite, shuddering at the cold against my bare legs.

Tom left me only moments before. We have one of those casual after-school arrangements, the sort of thing where we're both into it but neither of us will let on. It's a matter of face. Never look like you're that interested. He deliberately accidentally found me at lunch time and bantered for a while before delivering the line: 'You coming to the park after school?' Everybody knows what that means, but I said only that I might be. I showed up fifteen minutes late to find him on a swing, trying hard to be cool. He didn't waste his time, had his hands on my bum and started kissing me as soon as I got near enough. I run my tongue round my mouth. His taste is still there, chewing gum and unbrushed teeth.

I take out my phone to text him, then change my mind and text Claire instead. She'll want to know what happened so she can bitch to the others about it. She's a cow, but what do I care? Another two years and she'll be fat and pregnant and living in Ballysally and I'll never see her again. I pull my skirt down as far as I can over my thighs and shove my hands into my jacket pockets, delving deep for any traces of warmth I can find. It wouldn't kill them to have some heat on in this bus station. Maybe then they'd get a better class of customer.

All around me I can hear hissing as one by one the other buses release their brakes and depart. Still no sign of our driver. Bored and hungry, I wander over to the railing to watch the Friday-evening train pull into the station opposite. I like trains. They're glamorous in a drab sort of way. Not that Northern Ireland Railways is particularly exciting, but at least it carries the possibility of somewhere different, even if it is only Dublin. I hear the guard slam the doors with real venom as if to prevent anyone from making a break for it. That's something else I'm going to do as soon as I'm old enough – escape. The train chugs across the level crossing and an air of abandonment settles over the station. God, I hate this place.

At long last the bus driver strolls up, metal box in hand. His face is dour, his demeanour resentful as if someone has stolen his dreams. For years I've been getting this bus and he still pretends not to recognise me. Maybe he had a miserable childhood, or his wife decided she couldn't take it anymore and left with the kids. If he's anything like this at home I wouldn't blame her. I show my pass and head for my usual seat, seven rows back on the right-hand side, beside the heater. I stretch out my legs and relax as the warmth seeps up through my body.

The bus pulls back from the stand with a shudder and heads out into the night. Through the window I can just make out Venus, the only star I know. It's not technically a star but I find it reassuring to know it's there. We travel along narrow streets, past row after row of terraced houses and down the hill before crossing the river and heading west. It always amazes me that no matter where you are in the world the sun always sets in the west. It's the same for everyone. A bit like death, I suppose.

We have one last stop to make. Every night it's the same. Outside the old courthouse on the Castlerock road a man gets on. Late thirties or early forties, he wears the same grey jacket and trousers and the same resigned look. He buys the same ticket every night, too, a single to Limavady – a journey into eternity, stopping at every village and lay-by as the bus struggles round the coast. I am fascinated by him, by the sense of disappointment that clings to him like a worn-out coat that he hates but can't afford to throw away. It makes me wonder how he ended up like that.

The driver accelerates into the night. There is little traffic and we travel quickly, an illuminated lozenge bright against the blackness outside. The glare of the fluorescent strip above makes it difficult to see the shadows that flit by like spectres on either side of the road. Bored, I make faces at my own reflection in the yellow pane.

The lights at the level crossing begin to flash as the bus turns towards the village so we stop. It's always the same, caught on the wrong side of the tracks. One by one, the passengers dismount from the train and hurry away towards waiting cars. I wonder who they are, these total strangers who have temporarily shared each other's lives and who are unaware that their stories have briefly intersected with mine.

The barriers lift even before the train has left the station and we drive down to the seafront. It is a dead end, the village caught between the station and the coast, brought into existence solely because somebody decided it was a good place to build a railway line. The place feels deserted most of the time, but that's what happens when your inhabitants are always in transit to somewhere else. Somewhere better. The only thing I like about where I live is the sea. I like the unrestrained force of it, the way it reminds you just how insignificant you are in comparison with the elemental strength of nature. Tonight the sea looks black and menacing, raging against the dunes and the sea wall like an aquatic Sisyphus, doomed to eternally repeat its struggles. In the distance the Greencastle lighthouse blinks reassuringly, warning of hidden dangers, and beyond that – nothingness until you reach America. One day I'll go there and lose myself in its vastness.

We recross the railway line and this time take the back road out of the village, the bus twisting left then right as the driver negotiates the sharp bends. The ruins of the Earl Bishop's castle look down from the cliff top, standing guard over what was once its demesne, the temple poised between sea and land, the strand where he raced thoroughbred horses in the summer, the chapel he built so his servants would have somewhere to worship. I like history when it's like that. Real. Apparently the RAF were stationed in the castle during the war and one night they burned it down. Probably no-one noticed. It was a time when all the world was on fire. Now it's only a memory, a story to tell tourists and school kids. You're not supposed to go into the ruins, but, of course, everyone does. People are like that: tell them they can't and they do. But it keeps the place alive somehow. There's talk of rebuilding it one day, getting a grant from Europe and building a visitor centre. But it won't be the same.

My stop is at the crossroads. I step out carefully onto the silence of a broken pavement, and in the darkness I feel the grass and earth pushing up through the fragmented flagstones and clutching at my ankles. The bus pulls away, its red tail-lights disappearing down the steep hill. I look up at the cold, clear night. In the stillness I can hear the sea breathing, and it feels like the end of the world.

I wait until a solitary car passes, then I cross the road, its dips and curves familiar under my feet as I walk. In the pitch dark I can become invisible, anonymous. Only sounds exist. My breathing loud in the silence. Next door's dog pulling against its chain. Branches from the over-grown hedge clawing at my hair as I feel for the bolt on our gate. I fumble in my pocket for my key.

Somebody inside turns on a light and an orange glow reclaims some of the darkness. My father opens the door.

'I heard you coming. Good day? Dinner's ready.'

I drop my bag in the hall and take my seat at the table where I have eaten for the last fifteen years.

'You're late enough.' My mother's first words are a state-ment rather than a question.

'I went downtown with a few people after school. Then the bus got held up at the level crossing.'

'Guess who I saw hanging around the park with Tom Brady?' my brother interjects.

As ever, I ignore him. I decided long ago he wasn't worth the breath.

'He's a nice lad,' says my mother. 'I met his aunt the other day. Apparently his sister's doing very well at Cambridge.'

I roll my eyes and keep eating. I hate the banal conversations they have, all the mundane enquiries and mindless platitudes about dental appointments or second cousins or the cat's health. I eat as quickly as I can then shove my plate in the dishwasher and escape to my room. Everything is as I'd left it: bathrobe on the bed, books over the floor, curtains open. I go to close them then stop. The moon has emerged from behind a cloud and hangs in the sky as if suspended by an invisible thread. The temple stands silhouetted against the night sky like some intricate relic from another age. I'd barely noticed it when I got up this morning. Now it seems transformed.

I kick off my shoes and fling myself down on the bed, hands behind my head. Inconsequential murmurs drift up from the kitchen below and I reach over and turn the stereo on to drown them out. The night's blackness looks in at me as I lie there, seductively winding its way through my thoughts. The imprint of his hands on my skin. The feel of his body solid against mine. I slip my hand under my blouse, trace my fingertips across my belly, imagine his weight on me.

My mother's voice wakes me. 'You all right in there? You're very quiet.'

'Yeah, I'm fine, Mum. Just reading something.'

I listen until her footsteps grow faint, then I hurriedly close the curtains. Lying back down on the bed, I stare up at the ceiling. Ancient paper butterflies hang there, constructed one afternoon by my youthful self. I stand up and carefully peel off each one, picking every scrap of Blu-Tack off with my fingernails until it is completely blank. I throw the rubbish in the bin and take out my phone.

Night Breath

She lets her tight denim jacket fall open and folds her arms under her breasts. From the corner of her eye she sees him sidle cautiously towards her. Come on, she thinks, come on. At the last moment, shame pierces the darkness of his desires and he turns away. Before she can react, before she can draw him beyond the fringes of his fear, he is gone, scurrying back towards the normality of the brightly lit bars that call raucously from the other side of the square. Disgusted, she leans back against the park railings and feels in her pocket for the cigarette she has saved from earlier. Inhaling deeply, she flicks the ash in the gutter with as much contempt as she can muster.

It is a warm summer's night in the square. The parking spaces around her are filling like squares on a crossword puzzle as cars empty their contents onto the warm pavement, then settle down together for the night. Couples, businessmen, tourists discreetly disentangle themselves from air-conditioned interiors, adjust ties and scarves and drift off in search of a night's entertainment. Hurriedly, they pass her by, feigning not to notice her as she stands waiting for business.

Tired and bored, she abandons her vigil and walks the short distance to the dark, silent church that stands sentinel at the junction of two nearby streets. Sometimes it is open and she can shelter inside, can huddle against one of the huge metal radiators that squat penitentially at the end of each pew. But tonight when she tries the doors she finds them locked and she swears in frustration before slumping forlornly on the steps. She remembers the sense of wonder she once felt as, bedecked in her first communion dress, her gloved hands pressed together, she waited patiently for God's grace to descend. Another cheap story, she thinks as she picks herself up and pulls her skirt down over her thighs. Her sense of disappointment in God and his cassocked servants burns still. Yet more men who demanded submission, then failed to live up to even her most meagre expectations.

She turns and makes her way as nonchalantly as she can towards a row of clubs two streets away. From each door music stumbles drunkenly out into the night and garish lights fall like an unholy grace on those forced outside with their cigarettes. A few patrons leer and mutter obscenities as she passes, but she has long ago learned that drunks make dangerous customers. Instead, she makes her way towards some steps which descend to a cellar entrance. A set of muscles in a cheap, dandruffed suit blocks her path.

'Beat it, love. Nobody's interested here.'

'One drink. Ten minutes, that's all.'

'I told you, fuck off. If anyone wants you, they know where to find you.'

'Jesus, just one bloody drink.'

'Fuck … off. Or do you want me to call the Guards?'

She pulls her jacket closer and shuffles back up the steps. A night breeze has begun to brush against the branches above her and as she makes her way slowly towards the park she smiles at the sound of the leaves rustling against each other as if exchanging innumerable tiny caresses.

Her hand runs along the iron railings that surround the darkened park and she can sense spectral faces peering at her from passing cars, wondering if she is indeed what she appears to be. If she could charge for every lecherous look that had stroked her breasts or lifted the hem of her skirt, she would be a wealthy woman. But such men were mental thieves, bereft even of the coward's courage, stealing what they were afraid to pay for. Occasionally she turns and shouts at them, then laughs as heads bow and eyes are hastily averted.

The clock above the park gates warns that it is almost two o'clock. For almost three hours she has been standing there, unused, cold and hunger clawing relentlessly at her insides. She sits down on the pavement, as if in surrender, and thinks about calling it a night.

It is then that she sees him, a middle-aged man lurking under one of the beech trees whose branches hang low over the park railings as though begging for alms from passers-by. He is in his late forties or early fifties, she guesses, and for a few moments she is reminded of one of those old men who sit under trees waiting for some unseen spiritual rain to fall. She wonders if he is a Guard looking for a freebie, or a clergyman desperate to save her soul with his own. Then he moves out from the shadows and she sees he is just another punter in a grubby sports coat and scuffed shoes. In her desperation she makes it easy for him.

'Looking for some company?' she calls, making her way towards him. She touches his elbow encouragingly with her breasts and as he looks at her she sees excitement contend with fear on his face.

'Look, I've never done this before ...'

The same old lie.

'You leave this to me, then. We'll go to my place.'

She links her arm in his as though they are lovers and leads him towards her flat. On the way she outlines the details of their transaction as quickly as she can: what he can do, for how long, and how much. He nods in agreement, gathering his embarrassment around him like an old coat. Occasionally a head turns, but she hurries on, anxious to reach the flat before he changes his mind.

As she opens the door she whispers for him to keep the noise down, that her girlfriend is asleep in the next room. He steps back, frightened, but she closes the door quickly before he can escape. 'It's all right,' she says. 'Don't worry.' She moves briskly through the drabness into the room beyond and switches on a small bedside lamp. All the while she keeps hold of his hand, fearful lest he be swept away on a tide of his own guilt. She shrugs off her jacket to reveal a flimsy vest, then leads him to the bed. With a practised hand she unzips his trousers. Minutes later she feels the shudder of death go through him, and when she puts her head back she sees he is looking at her with what she thinks is guilt. She pulls his hand onto her breasts, but he draws away.

'No, don't. You've done enough.'

For a moment she sits, feigning disappointment, then stands and lets him watch her as she moves to the window and looks out. Beyond the blackened rooftops and orange streetlights, the threadbare sky shows a thousand points of light and she senses tranquillity begin to settle on the slumbering city. Perching herself upon the windowsill, she feels the coolness of the night air slowly enter her, and soon only the strange voice in the distance stops her from fading away completely.

'You must hate people like me. Punters, I mean.'

She looks at the grey figure standing next to her in the half-light. 'Why? You're paying for it.'

He doesn't reply.

She watches with disinterest as he stares at the ground, avoiding her gaze, and wonders if she can persuade him to pay extra. Before she can speak he asks the question they all ask.

'So how come you're a whore?'

'Because people like you pay me to be and I need the money.' She takes his hand and leads him to the bed. 'Now, how would you like something a little more interesting? Something special. It'll only cost a little more.'

'Can't you get a job or something?' he persists. 'Something to keep you from all this?' He gestures at the drabness around him and she feels a sudden flash of hatred.

'Do you think I'd do this if I had an option? It was just the way things turned out, that's all. I had too many dreams, too few prospects and thirty-eight-inch tits. Some people end up selling the *Big Issue*, but I ended up selling myself.'

She senses pity, or at least curiosity, and in the darkness tells him of a childhood in Mayo, of a beach where she'd run and play and where the surf would rush like a long-lost sister into her outswept arms. She tells him, too, of a father and a farm – a farm of rocks and thistles and frustrated hopes – and of the accident that finished off what the land had begun; how she had left to find money and how it had all come to an end in a tiny bedsit where her dreams had given way to the fantasies of others.

He remains silent throughout this story of hope and degradation, oblivious to the night-calling of cars and boats from the world beyond. With satisfaction she puts out her hand and feels the excitement that her lies have, as usual, engendered. She takes off her clothes.

When he is finished, she allows herself to look at the scar which mutilates his face, a tiny bicycle track that runs from forehead to chin. Without it, she thinks, his features would be quite passable, almost good-looking. A man not so much ugly as maimed.

'How'd it happen?' she hears herself ask.

In an instant his mood changes and she senses hatred harden like glass across his damaged face. She holds her breath.

'Don't pity me,' he hisses. 'I haven't paid for that. If I want pity I'll go to a priest, not a whore.'

He turns away and for a few moments only the hands on the clock dare move.

Eventually she feels his body relax and she puts her hand on his arm. 'There's no point in thinking about it. You just get on with it. You have to do that, don't you? In order to keep your sanity, in order to survive. Have you got a girlfriend?'

She feels his body go rigid once more and his hand pulls her face close to his. 'Who'd look at me? Who in the name of Christ would look at me?'

The violence that lies within him wakens from its slumber and her fear returns. Cautiously, she runs her hand ever so gently along his furrowed face, then kisses his scar.

After he has gone, she hides the money and goes to the bathroom to rinse her mouth. She reaches up to the top of the cabinet above the sink and feels about for the treasure she has hidden there. A small plastic bag. Just enough for tonight. She perches a candle on the side of the bath, lights it, and slowly taps the crystals into the pipe. As the flame warms the bowl, she inhales the vapour and feels her body lay down its burdens and relax. Taking a deep breath, she blows out the candle and tiptoes gently into the other room.

A small form lies sleeping in a single bed. Resting her head on the pillow, she feels the breath from two small nostrils like a tiny, thrilling breeze upon her face. In the imperfect silence she finds herself saying 'Ssshhh' to the ticking clock, and to the murmuring pipes, and to the distant calling of the city outside.

And as she falls asleep, her breath slips like a night breeze past a solitary figure, walking alone through the darkened streets, and passes over the Liffey where the waters flow darkly under the Halfpenny Bridge. On and on it goes, past the suburban home where she grew up, and where her father and mother sit waiting for a daughter they will never see again, and so on into the night until it mingles with the breath of the earth itself.

Promises

I run up the hill as quickly as I can, high heels stabbing futilely at the tarmac path that leads to my past. Determined to avoid being early, I've delayed too long and, as the cathedral's bells toll impatiently, I curse my stupidity on this of all days.

Inside, I excuse and elbow my way through a crowd reluctant to part lest it lose its hard-won view of the altar. The entrance hymn draws to a close and in the imperfect silence I at last find a space amidst the other latecomers who stand huddled just inside the door. The rows of pews in front of me are lined with solemn figures cut, it seems, from black crepe paper, and I stand on tiptoes to try to see if there is anyone I recognise.

'In the name of the Father and of the Son and of the Holy Spirit ...'

The priest intones the forgotten formulae of my childhood and I recall, for one brief moment, my youthful wonderment at the comforting certainties of faith. The people in front of me take their seats and, leaning forward, I pick out the familiar profiles from among the crowd. They look older than I'd imagined them to be, their faces creased and worn by the passing of years but each still recognisable. Stephen. Cathy. Claire. Jim. I recite the roll call of my youth, duly marking them present at the reunion I never thought I'd attend. It's been twenty years since I've seen most of them, but none will be surprised to see me. Not at John's funeral.

The service passes, an anaesthetic of ritual, the congregation's collective pain soothed by the comfort of repetition. Only his wife's final eulogy lifts the veil of detachment behind which I had vowed to shroud my feelings. I'd met her once at a college garden party and even back then was struck by how controlled she seemed, as if determined to adhere to the appearance of a happy marriage at all costs. I listen as she relates a familiar anecdote of their life together, an inconsequential story that I heard first from his lips, and in spite of myself I begin to smile as I remember a time that was never what I thought it to be.

**

A promising poet, he had just begun his tenure when I arrived and his appointment was a real coup for a college anxious to secure some publicity and attract new sponsors. I was as intrigued as every other undergraduate by the aura that surrounded him, though for form's sake we hid our excitement behind masks of indifference. In the college bar I joined in half-heartedly as my friends poked fun at his intellectual's polo neck and redundant scarf. Call it hindsight if you wish, but even then I felt there was something about the way he looked at me. Half-listening to the banter of students drunk on wine and knowledge, I wondered if he was sizing me up, assessing my talent as a potential player in some drama which he had yet to write.

For all that, we had little to do with each other during those first few months. I handed in a paper each week, then diligently discussed Elizabethan poetry, the Augustans, Yeats, for an hour in a room that smelled of stale coffee and second-hand books. Of course, I got round eventually to reading his collection of poems – *Autumn Onions*

– one wet afternoon in Blackwell's café, flicking through its thirty-two pages with studied nonchalance before purchasing it. The reviews on the back cover spoke of 'a subtle exploration of love and loss', but most of the poems I read were bleak descriptions of sex in sparsely furnished rooms or cars with torn seats, desolate and nihilistic encounters devoid of hope.

At our next tutorial, I struggled to focus on Shakespeare's sonnets and finally asked him straight out.

'What made you write poetry?'

'Vanity.'

'No, really.'

He paused in a way that would become so familiar and smiled what I took to be an embarrassed smile. 'I don't really know. Maybe it was a need for truth and honesty, whatever the hell those are. Or maybe I just enjoyed being pretentious. There was a time when I got a thrill out of telling people I was a poet.'

'You know, they're not bad, your poems, particularly the early ones.'

'Any favourites?'

'The dirty ones.'

We both laughed, conscious that we were straying onto a dangerous path. At the end of the class he stopped me, arm outstretched across the doorway like the tape that marks out a crime scene. I pushed against it with my chest and waited to see what he'd do.

'Why don't you call round to my rooms later and we can chat some more? I can show you some rough drafts if you like.' It was a pathetic line, but he wrote – and looked – better than he spoke, so I agreed.

That was how our affair started. Every Friday evening, provided his wife was away or at work, we'd meet and talk about poetry or life or whatever else sufficed for verbal foreplay, and eventually we'd end up in bed. This was where he was at his most creative and his most despairing. Lying there with him, even in the early days, the bed felt empty, as intimate and as vast as a poem.

**

The priest calls upon us to offer each other the sign of peace and as the man beside me turns and offers me his hand I realise for the first time what I've lost. Incense wafts through the confined air and I feel as if I am about to choke. I do not watch as the coffin is carried out.

Eventually, I follow the other mourners into the cold, harsh January light. As my eyes adjust to the piercing brightness, I begin to make out groups of mourners gathered like pickets at some spiritual strike, and soon I am assailed by the exuberant hugs and kisses with which we all try to recapture the carelessness of our student days. John would have scoffed, would have laughed it off as hypocrisy, but secretly he would have been pleased to see so many former colleagues and students there, so many friends and fellow writers, the people who were the backdrop to our years together.

I remember it now as a time of excitement and deceit, racing through invisible mazes and trying to hide where all could see. Once we made love in her bed – their bed – on a mattress which bore the imprint of her body. And as we lay there, naked and breathless, I imagined the sheets still warm from her presence.

'Were you ever in love with her?' I asked. I never said her name.

He stared at the ceiling as though an answer were to be found in the magnolia-painted expanse that passed for heaven that afternoon.

'At the start I suppose, when we first met. But even back then it was more about expectations. Everyone expected us to be together, even ourselves, and before we knew it we were trapped. Or at least I was, entombed in a world that I'd helped to create but had never wanted. That was why I stopped writing. Because I'd stopped living.'

'Are you living now?'

There was no answer. Twenty minutes later we dressed silently and left. That night in the college bar I saw him really drunk for the first time.

The six semesters that followed were filled with the heights and depths that form the jagged contours of relationships such as ours. We made love as often as we could until it became as tedious as an assignment, and I realised that his need for sex was a quest for affirmation, for validation, and that he could only find it in the body of a younger woman. Did he exploit me? Of course, but back then it didn't seem to matter. What was important was that we were together, and on the good days life felt better than it had ever been.

Still, there were some terrifying moments, like the afternoon his wife arrived home unexpectedly while I was in the shower, or when my roommate found him asleep in our dorm in the middle of the day. There was even an unsigned letter sent to the Dean, which detailed our indiscretions. Eventually came more public scandals – the drunken scenes at an undergraduate reception, a college fundraiser, a graduation ceremony where a cabinet minister was present. I can't be sure when precisely I first saw through him, when I first realised he was indeed the failure he claimed to be. But when the college, keen to avoid further embarrassment, arranged a sabbatical so that he could get treatment I was relieved. On our last night together he was too drunk, too alone, and I watched with cold contempt as he staggered off into the darkness. Twenty years later my husband left me for one of his grad students and I wrote to John. That was how I discovered he was dying.

**

It's a slow, hard mile up the hill to the cemetery. As we enter the gates, the grave lies open ahead of us, the gaping hole of its presence marring the clear morning. The plot is at the top of a slope with a clear view of one of the pubs he used to frequent. I smile. It's just what he would have wanted.

I force my way through the crowd, determined to be there at the very last, and as the box is lowered into the ground, I, too, throw a handful of earth into the blackness. Around me, others stand and weep, but I turn away. It is not quite over.

Early the next morning I return, treading carefully on the now frosty ground. Snowdrops have struggled into bloom along a nearby verge. I leave the path and crunch my way through the silence to where he lies.

He'd once made me promise to visit his grave. I was to come alone and I was to leave one thing in memory of him. A single red rose. It was a hopelessly romanticised gesture and, looking back, I can only assume he was drunk when he decided on it, but I'd made a promise and I would carry it out. I hold the stem tightly, relishing the sharpness of its thorns in my palm. There is no marker, just yesterday's wreaths masking the fresh earth. Strewn on top of them are three other flowers. Three other red roses. I throw mine on top of the others.

My Last Murder

Murders are always the same. We hover like vultures, alert to any sign of distress, waiting to pick a few quotes from a grieving relative or grim-faced clergyman, then dusting off the clichés five minutes before deadline.

I've lost count of the number of mornings I've stood guard before a ribbon of police tape, stamping my feet on cold concrete with the rest of the hacks at the 'scene'. Every so often a passer-by will stop to sightsee, drawn like a shark to the scent of blood; occasionally a forensic expert swathed in sterile white will pass under the tape and plod methodically out of sight, and for a few moments there'll be a scuffle as photographers vie for the best angle for their shot, lenses clicking like empty pistols in the cold air. Then they'll resume their conversations until some new detail – a brown evidence bag, a wreath, the local priest – provokes the feeding frenzy once more.

It was on a morning as ordinary as all the others that I found myself standing with Raymond and the others at the entrance to a lane on the outskirts of the town. Even in daylight it was a lonely place, one side flanked by the railings of a local high school and the other fringed by an overgrown hedge. I knew it as a shortcut frequented by joggers and dog-walkers in the mornings and by teenagers with cans of cider at night, a suburban no-man's land that residents complained about but no-one seemed to own.

That morning, police had cordoned off the entrance so that even with his most powerful lens Raymond couldn't see past the bend that lay fifty yards beyond the tape, so we were left to grumble and grouch and indulge in black humour as we watched forensic equipment being ferried up and down the lane. Rumour had it the victim was a young girl, but the police would confirm nothing until she'd been ID'd. Cold and hungry, I gathered reaction from the onlookers and coaxed a few quotes out of the school principal, then rattled off a few pars for the early edition. The location made the story – that and her youth. 'Girl's Body Dumped Beside School' would be my headline – and that of countless others.

By half ten, a selection of councillors had joined us, ever-conscious of the need to be seen and to be heard paying their respects to the lost daughter of potential voters. I did a bit with each of them, recording their well-meaning platitudes with disinterest masked by journalistic impartiality. Of course the night's murder was the last thing anyone expected. The community was in shock, their thoughts and prayers with the victim's family. Anybody with information should go to the police so the monster responsible could be brought to justice. Off the record, the word was that the vic was only fifteen or sixteen, a girl from one of the rural districts. Devlin, or maybe Dillon. Good people, farmers. A terrible tragedy.

The clatter of trolley wheels on uneven concrete sent me scurrying for a good vantage point among the photographers clustered at the lane's end, their cameras poised in morbid anticipation. Two paramedics pushed an empty trolley up the lane and returned a few minutes later with what remained of a life. As they loaded their burden into the back of the ambulance, I was struck by how sordid and yet solemn it seemed, the body barely there under a crumpled sheet like a pile of dirty linen on wash day. Behind us, a crowd had gathered, transfixed by the grim reality of the scene. One woman blessed herself, then hurried on with her shopping bags as if afraid she might be called upon to play a part in the grim drama being enacted before her. I was already writing my opening line in my head. *The town centre was brought to a standstill yesterday morning as people paid their respects to the schoolgirl whose body was dumped on Long's Lane.*

We were about to leave when I noticed a besuited figure emerge from a police car. I nudged Raymond. 'Over there, that's our man. Looks as if he's about to say something.'

We hurried over and I worked my way to the front of the scrum, Dictaphone aloft, ready for the statement. He waited until we were all in position, then cleared his throat.

'Name for the tape, please,' one of the cameramen shouted.

'Detective Inspector John Armstrong,' he said slowly. 'I'll read a short statement and then take a few questions.'

No-one answered lest they spoke over what might be vital first words. Taking a piece of paper out of his pocket, the Inspector began to read.

'A murder investigation has been launched into the death of a fifteen-year-old girl. Her body was found in the location behind me, known locally as Long's Lane, at about a quarter past seven this morning. We believe the victim was beaten and sexually assaulted, possibly by one or more persons, at some time between ten o'clock last night and seven this morning. We are appealing for the public's help in solving this most brutal of crimes and want anyone who may have information that might lead us to her killer or killers to contact us directly at the station or to use the confidential telephone.'

'Have you identified a suspect yet?' someone shouted.

'We're following a number of lines of enquiry and are confident we will find those responsible. But as I've already said, we need the public's help to do so.'

'Why do you believe there was more than one attacker?' I called out.

He paused to consider his answer. 'As this is an ongoing investigation, it would be inappropriate for me to comment further at this stage, but the nature and extent of her injuries, as well as other evidence, leads us to believe there may well have been more than one assailant.'

'Can you give any more detail as to the victim's injuries?'

A police press officer appeared from nowhere and blocked the microphone with her clipboard. 'That's all for the moment. We'll keep you updated via the police news line. Thank you all for coming.'

'Did you see his reaction when I asked that question?' I said to one of the other journalists as we turned away. 'There's clearly something they're not telling us. You heading up to the house?'

'God no, far too early for the BBC to doorstep the family. I'll have a word with the priest, put in a request through him. That's my limit. What about you? D'you have an address?'

'One of the councillors said he thought they lived up beyond the chapel in Milltown. It won't be that hard to find.'

'Do you know she was a pupil at the school there? I did a bit with the principal earlier.'

'Aye, so did I. He was great, a good talker.'

'Let me know if you hear anything.'

I waved as I got into the car. 'You too.'

**

I found the house easily enough. The village was one of those small rural communities where a few houses sit like enormous headstones around a pub and a shop. An elderly man putting out his bin directed me to a left turn a few miles beyond the village. Minutes later I found a square, solid structure set amid a scattering of outbuildings a few miles back from the road. There were no cars in the yard; I guessed everybody was at the mortuary but I knocked anyway, several times, just to make sure, and was answered by echoes that reverberated in the deserted house, then fled like ghosts around the hills. I gave up and headed back to the office.

It was the following day before I struck lucky. I'd been out on another story – a minister down from Belfast to cash in on the publicity due him for the construction of a new bypass – and on the spur of the moment decided to swing by the house again. This time the road was lined with cars; I abandoned mine on the verge and walked the last 500 metres. A wreath hung on the front door. As I walked towards it I reached into my bag and eased the switch on my Dictaphone to 'on'.

The door was open and I tiptoed gingerly inside. In a sitting room to the left of the hall I could see people huddled together, chatting quietly as though afraid the dead would overhear, and other lowered voices came from what I assumed to be the kitchen. As I stood there, suddenly uncertain, a middle-aged woman appeared from behind a door and looked at me expectantly. 'I'm sorry for your trouble,' I said and extended my hand. 'I just wanted to pay my respects.'

She put a tea towel down on the hall table and took my hand in hers. 'Thank you for coming, it's very good of you. I'm Kerry's aunt, Rosemary Wilson. Her mother's my sister.' Suddenly she stopped and I wondered if she suspected. 'I'm sorry … but I didn't catch your name?'

'Anne Doherty. I used to sub at Kerry's school. I'm afraid I only knew her in passing, but I wanted to come and express my condolences. She was a wonderful girl.' The platitudes came easily and a sense of relief – and then triumph – grew within me as I went unchallenged.

'You're very good,' she said, gripping my arm. 'But then, Kerry had that effect on people. They remembered her.'

I nodded in agreement.

'Your principal and some of the other teachers were here last night, though I'm afraid we weren't very welcoming.' She turned towards the stairs and motioned that I should follow. 'Kerry's upstairs.'

The room was painted a faded pink, the simplicity of its walls broken only by ragged posters which charted the dead teenager's progression from cartoons to Gothic romances to boy bands. Dining chairs had been brought in and lined up along the wall and there was a pile of presents, still wrapped, underneath the windowsill. 'I'm sorry. Do you mind me asking, was it her birthday?'

The aunt began to sob, then, with an effort of will, stopped and dabbed at the corners of her eyes with a tissue. 'I'm so sorry,' I said, putting my arm on hers. 'I didn't mean to upset you.'

'It's all right,' she said, sniffing. 'Yes, it was. She would have been sixteen yesterday.'

She began crying again, so I turned to the coffin. I had my headline: 'Teen Murdered On Sixteenth Birthday'.

The dead girl was pretty, her long blonde hair ringed with an Alice band that made her seem younger than her sixteen years. Perhaps that was how the family wanted to remember her, in happier times, in more innocent days. The white dress in which the body was clothed gave the girl the appearance of a bride, but one for which there would be no wedding day, no groom, no future. A faint red scar was visible near her hairline, the only sign of her violent death. She was as pristine as a waxwork doll moulded for the occasion, a mannequin rather than a person. I blessed myself and turned away from the coffin.

'She looks so peaceful. It must be so hard for you all.'

The aunt looked at me as if in search of something. 'It's been terrible.'

I nodded encouragingly.

'Losing a child is every parent's worst nightmare. My sister's just devastated and my brother-in-law ... well, she was his little girl. I don't know how they'll ever get over it. You could understand, accept it almost, if it was an illness or an accident, even if it was unexpected. They blame themselves for not doing enough about the bullying. But they didn't even know. My sister keeps saying she should have done something, but how could she when she didn't even know?'

It was at that moment I realised it might go national, that this sad, squalid little murder might be the making of me. Even as I stood there the copy began writing itself in my head as I tried to keep up the pretence with the aunt.

'I'm afraid I didn't know anything about that, I was only a substitute teacher and I only had Kerry a few times. I didn't know her well, but she seemed a lovely girl, very popular. I had no idea—'

'They all say they had no idea and they're all lying. They knew what was going on. Oh, they knew.'

She paused briefly to dab fresh tears with her tissue and I looked away while she composed herself.

'I'm sorry, I promised I wouldn't talk about it. It's just when I see her lying there ...'

Her words trailed off as she looked into the coffin and stroked Kerry's hair gently with her hand.

'I still can't believe that it happened. That it was *let* happen.'

I said nothing, and she apologised again.

'I'm sorry. It's not your fault. Here, let me get you a cup of tea.'

She took me back down the narrow staircase to the sitting room and pressed me with the weak tea and dry sandwiches that are the offerings we make to grief. I attached myself to a group of mourners near the door, middle-aged women in housecoats and tracksuits suddenly made important by the ceremony of death. 'It just goes to show you never really know what's going on,' one said. 'God knows what she was going through those last few months.'

'The poor child,' said another. 'What must it have been like for her? My Eimear says it was all over Facebook this morning, but apparently it's been taken down.'

She lowered her voice.

'The others are saying they lured her there. The bullies, I mean. They told her they wanted to make up, got her to come and meet them, then they attacked her.'

I put my teacup gently down on a nearby table and hoped fervently that my Dictaphone had recorded it all. 'Excuse me, I must go and pay my respects.'

The dead girl's mother and father sat expressionless on a sofa in the corner, too wrapped up in their own private hell to acknowledge the profusion of bodies that lined up to shake their hands. Two teenagers – presumably a brother and sister – stood behind them, thanking the mourners with the numbness of automatons as though whatever spark gave them life had died out of sympathy with their sibling. I gave my condolences along with the rest and was struck by how cold they seemed, the mother staring through me with eyes of glass.

When I got back, I headed straight for the editor's office. He was sitting at his desk, examining proofs on the computer, correcting the next morning's headlines.

'I got the family,' I said triumphantly.

'Good girl. How did you manage it?'

I'd spent the drive back preparing for this question. He had to ask, but I knew he didn't really want to know. The key was to be vague, to give him an 'out' in case anything went wrong, something to tell the owners if the lawyers came calling.

'The wake was on and they invited me in.'

I watched him size up the information and waited for his verdict. 'Well done. We've got our lead, then. We'll need to make up a new front. What's your top line?'

'Teen Murdered On Birthday By Bullies – Family'.

He nodded. 'I like the birthday line.'

'I know. Great timing, wasn't it? Couldn't have been better. Her presents were lined up beside the coffin.'

'Shame we don't have a pic. Let me know as soon as your copy's done.'

I wrote it up in twenty minutes and pressed submit.

It was an exclusive. The next day all the others went to the door, like actors in some macabre parade, but no-one else was allowed in, no-one else managed to penetrate the wall of grief and suspicion with which the family now surrounded itself. No-one else came close to my act of betrayal. The aunt rang when she saw the story and shouted down the phone at me for a good ten minutes.

'Where did you get that stuff about my niece, about my family? She's not even buried and you're writing that stuff about her. How dare you?'

'Why, is any of it untrue?'

'That's not the point and you know it. How dare you brazen your way into my sister's house like that?'

'Listen, I'm very sorry for your trouble, but if you remember, I was invited in.'

'You lied to me. You said you were a teacher at the school.'

I played my ace. 'I was. Until two years ago. I think I even taught Kerry once or twice. It's all true, you can check with the school if you like. If you'd asked me was I a reporter, I would have told you. Anyway, I've done you a favour. Look at the reaction this story's got. Now everyone knows what happened there might even be an official investigation.'

She hung up and I looked round to see the rest of the newsroom listening in grudging admiration.

I went to the funeral, taking a seat in a side aisle next to a statue of the Virgin Mary, half-listening as the priest intoned his way through the homily. The dead girl's brother and sister did the readings, enunciating their words with dignity and suppressed grief. The mother sat in the front pew, a broken figure, one hand barely resting on the smooth, polished wood of the coffin. Each time her daughter's name was mentioned, she would caress it, and it was with difficulty that her husband removed her arm from the coffin before the final procession.

I waited until everyone had left and soon the only sounds in the church were those of the sacristan as he gathered up the missalettes and picked up the forgotten gloves and scarves, the loose earrings and broken umbrellas that were the only reminder of the departed congregation. I wandered idly over to where the votive candles flickered, silent prayers that would never be answered, hopes that would fade, lives that would be extinguished and forgotten and replaced. And then, for some reason – not guilt, not pity, not faith – I lit a candle, then quickly, without looking back, hurried outside.

The Morrigan:
A Dramatic Monologue

I was born in the Bogside on 5 October 1968, a time and a place that have long since passed into history. The actual house was knocked down long ago and exists now only in documentaries and in the minds of those who were there. Back then, the Bogside was a community huddled together, seeking protection from the poverty and neglect that were their immediate landlords. Above them at the top of the hill, Derry's Walls kept a constant watch, a stone boundary where time had stopped at 1689.

Looking back now, I realise that all my childhood memories are strangely monochrome, as if somehow my life then was lived out within the confines of a black-and-white newsreel. Of course, if that were the case, I'd probably be less conscious of the blood, of the dark crimson stain which washed over and eventually seeped deep into the fabric of my life and the lives of so many others when the arteries of civilised behaviour were first cut. But I can't: I was born into it, and its currents have carried me along for much of my life.

That life began with the unlikely coupling of my father, Charlie Doherty, and Margie Thompson, preacher's daughter and Prod. Charlie claimed to be the owner of a haulage company, the Red Stag Line, but in reality he was a truck driver who drove an ageing ten-wheeler from Bantry

Bay to Malin Head with near-suicidal bravado. By 1968, however, this short, stocky man with an answer for everyone and a cigarette permanently clamped between his fingers, had become one of the country's most determined, courageous, and least well-known civil rights leaders – the movement's blue-collar champion – and for a time he was as well known as McCann and Cooper, Fitt and Hume. Indeed, had it not been for the camera angle, it would have been his face next to Bishop Daly's in that famous shot of Bloody Sunday, and it was that image most who showed up for his funeral eleven years later preferred. They were much less comfortable with the thought of an IRA volunteer killing and dying for Ireland's blood-drenched freedom. Perhaps they hoped it was a different man, or that my father's early record absolved him of responsibility for some unacknowledged and unacknowledgeable guilt.

My mother, Margaret – Margie – is still alive and owns a clothes shop, Stylus, on the Strand Road. It's the sort of place that caters for the more mature woman, and most of Derry's greying population will have passed through its doors at some point or other. Incredible as it may seem she was originally a Presbyterian from the Fountain but turned Catholic when she married my father some six months before my arrival. It was a courageous, not to say startling, decision at the time and one which eventually cost her both her family and her friends.

She told me of their first meeting only once, years later, when I was off school with tonsillitis. They met while she was attempting to bring Jesus to ignorant sinners on Ferryquay Street on a Saturday afternoon. My mother was far from devout – she often said she had the belt marks to prove it – but her father, a would-be lay preacher, had insisted his daughter accompany him on his conversionary activities. So there she was, standing on the corner at

Woolworth's, Bible in hand and Sodom and Gomorrah on her tongue, when my father drew up in his lorry and pretended to ask for directions. Ma was never one to drag her heels when the devil nudged her towards temptation, so when Charlie flashed his teeth (and God knows what else) at this prim and proper Presbyterian, she quickly slipped the spiritual leash and began to chat to him. She insisted that at first she only meant to give him directions – out of Christian charity, as it were – but Satan is a wily serpent and before she could tell him to turn left at the end of the street, she'd agreed to meet him that very night in Tracy's Bar at the foot of William Street.

What they got up to I have no idea, but the night ended with my father promising to drive his truck up to my mother's front door and ask her out. It was a courageous decision, given that in those days few Catholics ever ventured into the Fountain, and fewer still contemplated the kind of things my father had in mind for one of its dwindling number of daughters. The result was inevitable and predictable. After both they and my mother's family had endured a constant stream of insults, they left one night to a barrage of stones and bottles – a form of confetti highly fashionable at the time.

Six months later, my mother – now installed among her adopted people on Rossville Street – went into labour and was assisted in my subsequent delivery by our neighbour, Annie McCafferty. Dr Devine was typically late in arriving and I was unusually early so Annie – who had called in to borrow a cup of sugar – acted as midwife and was the first thing I caught sight of when I entered the world. My mother, despite the indignity of giving birth with the neighbours' kids gawking through the curtains, was to joke ever afterwards that due to the rioting, I was the only delivery made that day in the Bogside.

Not surprisingly, given that it was 5 October and the first barricades were being thrown up in the Bogside, my father was at that very moment leading a group of protestors seeking to prevent an RUC patrol from proceeding towards Rossville Flats and into an almost certain confrontation. He had just begun the first bars of *We Shall Not Be Moved* when news of my arrival ensured that, in fact, he would, and in his flight he sparked a general panic which gave the RUC one of its few successes in those early days of civil resistance. Indeed, I have always felt somewhat of a traitor at having broken up a civil rights protest with greater ease than a baton charge, and a sense of guilt still lingers at being the only thing ever to have caused my father to retreat in the face of danger.

Given the somewhat unusual circumstances of my birth, I sometimes disappoint friends and Americans by having to admit that my subsequent childhood was very ordinary. Of course, the Troubles were a constant backdrop to our lives. Armed soldiers patrolled our streets, helicopters hovered overhead and barbed wire grew up amongst us like a weed nurtured by our hatred. But I was a child of the Troubles and accepted the abnormalities of my upbringing as … well, normality. I played on streets which served as channels for a vicious, implacable hatred – a hatred which had been flowing for centuries and which was then once more at high tide. But back then I was to a large extent unaware of its significance and merely wondered, as children sometimes will, at its more outward manifestations. In every other respect I was a typical little girl, running around the Bogside in a gingham dress with a snotty nose and a battered doll, as mischievous and as thoughtful and as innocent as any other.

In the political maelstrom of the early Troubles, however, our home life grew increasingly chaotic. My father had given up the road shortly after I was born, ostensibly to spend more time with his new family, and had eventually found work at a local butcher's. But in reality, the thought of being away from Derry at a time of such upheaval had been too much for him. He joined the Citizens' Action Committee and in the years that followed played his part in the Battle of the Bogside and numerous other now forgotten confrontations. He was, I suppose, one of those men who had to be totally committed to everything he did. My mother used to joke that the only things he wasn't committed to were Gransha and his family, and when he wasn't out protesting or chopping up meat at the butcher's, he was down at Magee studying for a degree in politics and sociology.

In August 1971, when I was almost three, my father was interned, and for the next six months we lived without him. I was far too young to remember much about his enforced absence, but in any case my mother was the single most important person in my life. She is still one of the most accomplished women I have ever known. Hard working, thrifty, intelligent, reliable, dependable ... qualities which have enabled her to become one of Derry's most successful businesswomen. It was emotion that became the challenge as the pressures and frustrations created by my father's activities slowly drained away her capacity to care.

My father was returned to us for the momentous month of January 1972, and even though I know he was as committed to the cause as ever, he always managed to leave some time aside for us as a family. Every bank holiday, every feast day, every Chinese New Year – you name it, we celebrated it – the three of us would pile into his little Citroen 2CV and head off into Donegal in search of some new scenic or historic spot which one of his friends had told him about

over a pint of Guinness. He was, I suppose, an incurable romantic and would have looked for Glockamorra if he could
have afforded the petrol, or chased a rainbow if someone
had been daft enough to lend him a helicopter. And so, off
we went in search of the beautiful and the improbable –
fairy trees, Famine cottages, crashed World War II planes
– and sometimes we found them. At moments like that, my
father's eyes would glow with excitement and my mother
would laugh and untie the scarf with which she'd invariably
bound back her hair and allow its strands to blow like gos-
samer in the breeze. At times like that, I was – in fact, we all
were – truly happy.

Like so many others, the turning point in my father's
life would come on Bloody Sunday. As usual, he was near
the front of the marchers as they made their way down
our street, and my mother told me years later that he saw
four of the victims go down. As the bullets tore into the
crowd, he tried to get help for the wounded and dying, and
the feelings of utter helplessness he endured that winter's
evening as he stood in the street and watched the sky pale
over the scene of carnage seem to have radically and ir-
revocably altered his attitude.

Not even my mother knows precisely when he joined
the Provos, but by the late 1970s he was one of the most
active of all Republicans in the city. Reliable sources, as
I think they're called, have told me that he was on the
Command Staff of the Derry Brigade, and he was also one
of their chief bomb makers. How many men died at his
hands, and how many lives he destroyed, I do not know. I
loved him as my father, and, until comparatively recently,
neither knew nor cared if there were widows or orphans
who wore black because of him.

Throughout the period of my father's descent – or
conversion, if you will – into violent Republicanism, my

mother worked steadily at maintaining our home and developing her own potential as an individual. She had always been handy with a needle and thread, and after several years of making curtains and loose covers on a casual basis for friends, she opened a little shop on William Street. My father was by then too engrossed in his own activities to pay anything other than cursory attention to my mother's little venture into capitalism, and it was only as the years went by that he came to realise it had grown into yet another barrier between them.

Chief amongst these barriers, of course, was my father's increasing commitment to the Republican struggle. My mother had from the outset never really accepted the need for violence – two wrongs don't make a right, she would constantly say – and gradually she came to see the struggle for a United Ireland as a form of war against her own people, or at least her former people. Late into the night, they would argue over the morality of the latest IRA action. Republican extremism, my mother would declare, had turned a stream of protest into a torrent of blood, and it had to be dammed before we all were damned. My father, in frustration and incomprehension, would thump his fist on the kitchen table and explain once again that armed resistance was the only way to sever the link between England and Ireland and the only way to create lasting peace. Standing in the doorway, I began to realise that the only link being severed was the one between themselves.

During those years of increasing turmoil, it was my mother who was always there for me, but it was the times with my father that stood out. One in particular I remember very clearly. I was about six at the time. My mother and father were both out, so Mrs Bradley from two doors up was keeping an eye on me. It was a stormy night in November, the wind and rain howling to be let into the warmth, and in their frustration whining and scratching at every rickety window and every ill-fitting door. I lay awake in my bed, a book of fairy tales discarded on the floor and my mind filled with thoughts of pookas and banshees and witches' curses. And as I lay there, I began to imagine all the spooky things children conjure up when they can't sleep, like goblins lurking under the bed or my dolls coming to life. So I hid with the bedclothes over my head and waited for Daddy to come home.

To the back of our house was a row of trees which separated us from the bigger houses behind, and on stormy nights the wind would take one particularly large tree in its arms and lead it in a frenzied waltz of swirling, swishing extravagance, and its branches would dip down and catch in the street light and shadows would begin to dance on the walls of my bedroom. That night as I lay there terrified, I saw the shadow of the tree change shape, change into something solid and menacing. I began to scream, a child's scream, high-pitched and seemingly unheard amid the sea of sound outside.

Then my father rushed in and took me in his arms and kissed me and told me that there was nothing there, and even if there had been wouldn't he always be there to protect me? Pulling back the curtain, we peered into the blackness to where he pointed out a large piece of plastic sheeting which billowed like a sail or a shroud in the branches of the tree. And as we both began to laugh, I looked at the wall behind me and there, sure enough, was the shadow of the tree with its mantle draped over its left shoulder. And there, too, were my father and I, his shadow-body between me and the spectre thrown up by nature.

Given the passion with which my father approached everything he did and his growing estrangement from my mother, it is hardly surprising that a further factor in their continuing divergence was the series of affairs he had with other women. How much my mother knew of these I cannot say for certain, but by the end of the '70s I was old enough to realise that my parents were living almost completely separate lives. Most nights my father would leave the house at seven or eight o'clock and not return until the early hours, and my mother would sit quietly at the kitchen table sewing and drinking cup after cup of coffee while I got myself to bed. Sometimes I would wake at two or three in the morning to the sound of the front door opening and I would listen as my parents' footsteps met in the hallway. Then hers would sound resignedly on the stairs and his would echo in the empty kitchen, and I would sob quietly with relief and frustration.

By the time I was ten I had begun to take my mother's part in the battle of wills being waged between them. I was still very much my father's daughter insofar as I continued to look with hostility on the khaki-clad uniforms that patrolled our streets and whose voices sounded of a country that was not mine. But my mother's disapproval of violence had lodged in my mind and I had begun to ask myself if all those people who prayed for peace at Mass could be wrong. My father, when I asked him, would look at me with what I thought was indulgence but now believe was sympathy, and would explain again and again that in a war people had to do things they were subsequently ashamed of but had to do them anyway. Being ten – and suddenly wise in the ways of the world – I would know he was speaking of himself and I would walk quietly away and leave him with his dilemma.

I was not always so understanding, however, and at times I would take up the standard of abandoned child and confront my father with his increasing neglect. Often he would arrive home to find me standing in the hallway, hands on hips in imitation of my mother, demanding to know where he had been and why he hadn't thought of the dinner that had now been sacrificed to the gods of his selfishness. He would look at me with a straight, serious face, then sweep me up in his arms and ask me how his little spit-cat was, and had I attacked any boys yet. Soon we would be rolling on the floor in laughter and my mother would stand, sad-eyed and silent, watching from the kitchen.

It was to be the hunger strikes which were the turning point in all our lives. Looking back, it is easy to see that the crisis was in fact a watershed in the Troubles, but at the time, the most obvious manifestations were the riots and the killings that were to claim the lives of so many others. Among them would be my father.

By 1981, my mother had become a successful business-woman and early that year she moved into new premises on the Strand Road, a street which her husband had once regularly bombed. My father had become one of the key Republican leaders in the city and was regularly detained by the RUC or army. For my part, I was determined not to be pushed aside by the excitement of their new, separate lives and turned myself into a moral fury, regularly castigating them for their neglect of each other and of me.

One day, shortly after the last hunger strike was called off, I made my father promise to be home early so that we could all eat together. By nine o'clock he still hadn't returned and in my anger I hurled his dinner into the bin, plate and all. An hour later he slunk in, too tired to offer an excuse let alone an apology. To my shame, I tore into him, screaming like a banshee. *How dare he stand us up yet again! Today, of all days. I bet he didn't even remember it was my birthday. Yes – my birthday.* He looked shocked and for once I could see genuine repentance rush to his face, but I wasn't going to let him off that easily. *Oh, no. I told him straight. He never thought of me or Ma. Never thought of our happiness. He was too damn busy with the dead or dying to notice the living. Well, I was glad that the hunger strikers had died. I hoped more of them died.*

Then he struck me. Not the smack of admonition that he had sometimes administered as a punishment for childish misdemeanours but a proper slap across the face – the kind that turns the room around and splinters it into a thousand teary shards. In the shocked silence that followed we stood motionless, I with my arms by my sides waiting for a second blow, he with his hand in mid-air, staring at it as if it didn't belong to him, as if some supernatural force had taken possession of it and had used it against his will. I looked at him with as much loathing as I could muster and saw that my hatred hurt him more than his slap had hurt me. And then, without so much as an attempt at reconciliation, I walked away and savoured the sweet bitterness of blood on my tongue.

Things were never quite the same after that. We carried on as best we could, but blood had been spilled between us and words spoken that could never be fully retracted. In the world beyond the killings continued, soldiers and policemen and IRA volunteers dying in ever more pointless incidents as the Troubles struggled towards a conclusion few could have foreseen in the dark days of the 1980s.

My father died on a warm spring evening in 1983, a single bullet entering his chest and stopping a heart that was already broken, already drained by a struggle that had demanded too many sacrifices. In the years since his death I have come to see him as both victim and perpetrator, as a participant in an event that no-one planned and no-one prevented. Whether he turned his back on the future or helped to create it, I will leave others to decide. To me, he was simply my father and I his daughter, and all I can do is live each day aware of the need to make that mean something.